His & More Pleasures

By M.S. Parker

Copyright © 2015 Belmonte Publishing LLC
Published by Belmonte Publishing LLC.
ISBN-13: 978-1511853187

ISBN-10: 1511853182

Table of Contents

His Pleasures

Prologue

Rylan

I still couldn't believe it. Jenna Lang – the tough tattooed tech, the strongest and most amazing person I knew – was sleeping in my arms. I'd been intrigued with her from the first moment I'd seen her.

At first, I'd assumed it had been an admiration of her intelligence and skill at her job, but as that first night progressed, I'd seen that there was so much more to her than that. Her strength covered a vulnerability that made me want to protect her.

My arms tightened around her as I thought about how close I'd come to losing her tonight. No matter what she said, I still blamed myself for Christophe. My stomach twisted at his name. Rage flamed in my gut as I thought of the things he'd taken perverse pleasure in seeing her do.

I brushed back a strand of her hair and let my fingers trail along her cheekbone, just above the cut that bastard had given her. Most people looked at her and all they saw were the tattoos, the piercings and, of course, the bright blue hair. I had to admit, even I'd found myself caught off guard by the outer package. Now, it was just another one of the things that made her so amazing.

And I loved who she was.

I hated what had happened to her. I hated it so much that I wanted to hit something every time I thought about all the people who had hurt her. Hit and maybe worse. I wanted to beat the shit out of Christophe, but I had a feeling if I saw any of the men who'd abused her, I'd want to do more than just knock out a few teeth.

I closed my eyes and pressed my face against her top of her head, breathing in the scent of shampoo and soap, both mingled with smell that was uniquely her. I loved the way she smelled and I felt my body responding. If she hadn't needed her sleep, I would've woken her and made love to her until we were both too tired to speak. We had all weekend though and I could wait until morning to be inside her again.

Heat flushed through me as I thought back over the last couple hours. While I wished the circumstances that had brought us to this point had been different, I couldn't deny that the time that followed had been among the best in my life. I closed my eyes, picturing her face when she put her hands in mine and told me she trusted me.

The rest of the memory followed.

The taste of her, like nothing I'd had before, and the sound as she came apart around my tongue. I'd felt her muscles trembling under the soft skin of her thighs. When she'd told me to stop, I'd been terrified I'd hurt her. The thing I wanted more than anything was to protect her, to make sure no one ever hurt her again, and the moment I'd seen her tears, I'd thought I'd failed. Then she'd said she was too sensitive after having four orgasms and I'd been unable to hold back the surge of pride I'd felt. Pride that I'd been able to make her feel something good from an act that had once caused her such pain.

I shifted and my hand brushed against the side of her bare breast. I cupped the firm flesh and she stirred, a frown appearing on her face.

"Shh," I whispered. I pressed my lips against the top of her head. "It's okay. I have you." I kissed her temple. "You're safe, my love."

Slowly, so very slowly, her body relaxed against mine.

"I love you, too."

The words still echoed in my mind. I'd told her I would wait for her to say them, and I'd meant it. Hearing her response as I was above her, inside her, had almost made me come right there. I'd always prided myself on my control, and I hadn't finished prematurely since I was a horny sixteen-year-old groping my girlfriend in the back of my dad's car.

3

And yet, four words from this blue-haired beauty had almost done it. The memory made my cock harden, but I didn't try to will it away. Instead, I let myself remember...

Her pussy was tight around me as I told her to close her eyes. Mine stayed very open though. I wanted to see every emotion as it crossed her face, every minute change, every shift.

She was so beautiful that each time I saw her, my heart ached. As I thrust into her, determined to give her every last bit of pleasure I could, I watched her face. Watched as, impossibly, she became even more beautiful. I tightened my grip on her wrists, ever aware of how precious it was that she trusted me with this.

When she opened her eyes and I saw that the pale gray had darkened to the color of a sky just before a storm, my chest tightened. For the first time since I'd met her, there were no walls, no barriers. I could see everything she was feeling, all of the things she couldn't put into words. I understood every one, because I was feeling them too.

"Rylan," she murmured my name as she rolled toward me. She pressed her face to my chest as she snuggled more tightly against me.

I ran my hand up and down her back, feeling the scars beneath the angel wing tattoos. It had been a long time since I'd slept with a woman in my arms. I'd had lovers over the years, but in the last four years, none I'd allow to stay. It had been sex, nothing more. Nothing like this. In fact, only one had ever come close, and even Lara had never made me feel like this. She'd been the only long-term relationship I'd had... and things had ended beyond badly.

Chapter 1

– Four Years Earlier –

I was still in a daze as I walked into the hotel and booked a room. The desk clerk smiled at me and asked if I was here for the skiing. When I didn't reply, the smile faltered and I knew he was chalking me up as some rich kid asshole, but for once I didn't care.

Only the most expensive room was left and I took it. Why not? I was doing well – more than well if I was honest. After what I'd just seen with my own eyes, I deserved a bit of a splurge. Besides, what was the point of being a self-made millionaire if I didn't spend money on the things I wanted?

I still didn't understand what had happened. I'd known Lara Roache since she was seventeen and we'd started dating when she turned eighteen. Even though my sister and my best friend both told me it wasn't a good idea, I'd asked Lara to move into my apartment after just eight months.

We'd celebrated our two-year anniversary last week and I'd already started looking at rings. I figured an engagement at Christmas, then a year or two to plan the wedding. We'd still be fairly young to get married, but not crazy young.

I was already in the elevator when I realized I hadn't brought any clothes with me. All I had was the laptop bag I happened to have when I'd walked out of my place. It was a nice apartment, but lately we'd been looking into buying a house. After all, if Lara and I were going to get married, we'd wanted a place where we could raise a family.

I gave a bitter laugh and was thankful no one was in the elevator to hear. There was always the off chance someone would recognize me, and the last thing I needed was some tabloid story about how I was losing my mind or speculating why I was checking into a hotel.

I scowled. If it hadn't been for my partner, Curt, talking me into doing that interview with *People* for their "Hottest Under 25" article, no one would know who I was and I could've stayed in Fort Collins. Since the article's release a few days ago, everywhere I went, people talked to me. Never again. I'd told Curt he would be the public face of Archer Enterprises from here on out, and nothing short of death was going to change that.

I stepped off the elevator and breathed a sigh of relief that the hallway was empty. I was not in the mood to see people right now, even strangers. I was still trying to wrap my head around how my world had just completely spun off its axis in the last couple hours. I really didn't feel like having to play nice.

The room was top of the line, but I barely registered it. I didn't care about the room. I walked through the small sitting area into the bedroom and set my laptop bag next to the bed. I kicked off my shoes and started to strip down. I needed a shower. Maybe that could help erase the last few hours.

I cranked the hot water up as much as I could stand and stepped inside. I closed my eyes as I moved under the spray and tried not to think about what had happened. Of course, the memories came anyway.

I knew I had a stupid grin on my face, but I couldn't help it. My real estate agent had called just as I was leaving the office and wanted to know if I'd come by and see a house he thought was perfect for me. I'd told Lara I needed to work a couple hours over and now I was glad I had. It was going to be so much better to surprise her. I hadn't made an official offer, but this was the place. I could feel it in my bones. Six acres along a lake. An absolutely massive house with a beautiful interior. I could see us spending the rest of our lives in that house, raising children and growing old with Lara.

I'd made one more stop on the way home to pick up daisies, her favorites, and a bottle of wine to celebrate. When I didn't see her in the living room, I set the wine on the kitchen counter and the flowers next to it, then headed back toward the

9

bedroom. *My stomach tightened in anticipation. Sometimes, when I worked late, she'd head to bed in some sexy lingerie and wait for me to get home.*

I opened the door and all of my dreams shattered.

Lara was wearing sexy lingerie all right. A tight black corset that pushed her generous breasts up, but didn't cover the perky nipples. No panties, but garter belts that attached to sheer black thigh-high stockings. Her dark red hair was fanned out around her head and her features were contorted in pleasure. Between her legs was a shapely blonde I recognized as Cassandra, a twenty-something lawyer who lived two floors below us. Neither one of them appeared to have noticed me as Cassandra continued to go down on my girlfriend.

"Right there, baby. Yes, please. More. Lick me. Hard."

I couldn't do anything but stare as Lara came with a cry I'd thought was reserved for me alone. We'd both had lovers before we'd met, but we never talked about them. We'd said it was only going to be us.

"Oh shit!"

Cassandra's exclamation broke through my shock.

"Rylan."

Guilt lifted the tone of Lara's voice as she scrambled for her robe, but not half as guilty as I thought she should sound. I didn't even look at Cassandra as she grabbed her clothes and left the bedroom.

"What the fuck, Lara?" The words didn't come out as angry as I intended, but at least they didn't sound hurt. I was still pretty numb at the moment and I wanted to stay that way.

"Rylan, I'm so sorry." She climbed off the bed and walked toward me.

I shook my head and took a step back. "Talk, don't touch."

Her jade eyes glittered with tears and I felt a flare of anger. How dare she act upset? Like she was the one who caught me cheating? And like this! This wasn't like I'd seen her out to dinner with another man or kissing him. I'd fucking walked in on her getting eaten out by another woman.

"You know I'd been with men and women before I met you," she began and I could see her fingers tremble as she lifted them to her lips. "Then you and I were so good together and... well, you're such a great guy. I thought you were the one."

I couldn't believe what I was hearing.

"You're a great guy, Rylan, and that's what makes this so hard."

"No," I snapped. The anger was coming now and I struggled to reign it in. "You don't get to act like you're some victim, Lara. Not after this."

"It just happened," she said, tears spilling over. "I've been fighting against my attraction to Cassandra for months and then today, I was dressed up, waiting for you to come home and she knocked on the door—"

11

"What the fuck?" I cut her off. "I don't want to hear the rest. And do you really think it makes me feel better to know you've been attracted to her all this time?"

Her chin lifted and her mouth tightened in a defense I could see coming. "I can't help it," she said. "It's how I am." She softened and her eyes glistened again. "I care about you, Rylan, but if I can't love you like that, then I can't love any man. I'd always thought of myself as straight woman who'd experimented, maybe bisexual, but I can't deny it anymore." She gave me that sad look she used when she wanted me to see her way. "I'm a lesbian. There's nothing I can do about it."

I stared at her, unable to believe an intelligent woman could be so dumb. "You think that's what this is all about?" I waved my hand back and forth between her and the door. "I don't give a damn about what gender you want to fuck. You lied about it. You cheated on me, Lara. Just because you wanted Cassandra didn't mean you had to fuck her right then and there."

Her pale skin flushed.

"In our bed!"

I began to pace, waiting for her to say something, anything. When she didn't, I turned to her and continued, "When you first started thinking this, you should've told me." I ran my hand through my hair. "You know what, it doesn't matter anymore. We're done." I looked around. "I can't be here right now. Take the weekend, get your shit

12

together and get out."

"Rylan." She reached out her hand and then dropped it. "I really am sorry."

I sighed, suddenly exhausted. "Someday I might be ready to hear that, but it's not tonight."

"Dammit!" I slapped my palm against the side of the shower. "Damn you, Lara. Why couldn't you have just told me?"

By the time I got out of the shower, I didn't exactly feel better, but I wasn't worse, so I accepted it.

Lara had been my only serious girlfriend. I'd dated girls on and off in high school and college, but I'd always been so busy with work that it never got beyond casual. By the time I was nineteen, I'd even gone away from casual dating to random hook-ups.

That's how I'd met Janice, the CSU grad student who'd introduced me to a whole new way of playing during one extremely intense and exciting weekend. Then, at an S&M party, I'd seen Lara, another student at the college who I'd spoken to once or twice in passing.

My phone rang, pulling me out of my thoughts. I frowned. The only person who'd be calling me this late would be Lara and I really didn't want to talk to her again. I felt a wave of relief when I glanced at the screen. It wasn't Lara.

"Hey, Suzette." I kept my tone light. No need for her to know what was going on.

"Rylan!"

I couldn't help but smile. Suzette was six and a

half years younger than me, my half-sister through our dad. For the first couple years of her life, I'd been with my mother, who'd gone to great lengths to keep me away from my father and his new family. She even changed my last name to her maiden name when she changed hers back. I found out later that she'd threatened to take my dad to court if he didn't agree to let my last name be changed from Dougall to Archer.

When I was twelve, my mom went off the deep end and the shit really hit the fan. Long story short, she ended up losing primary custody of me and I went to live with my father, step-mother, and half-sister. I'd known what changing my last name back would do to my mom, so I'd kept it, which hadn't made my father happy. That was the story of my life, constantly torn between my parents. My one bright spot, however, had always been Suzette. I adored my little sister.

"What are you doing this weekend?" She didn't bother with any small talk.

"Nothing," I said and fell back on the bed.

"Since we have a three-day weekend, some friends and I are heading up to the cabin first thing in the morning. You and Lara should come too. I haven't seen you in forever."

"Lara and I broke up," I said, my voice as flat as if I'd been reporting the weather.

"Oh, Rylan, I'm so sorry. I know you really liked her."

I didn't bother to correct her and say that I'd

loved Lara, so much that I'd been planning on marrying her before I'd caught her fucking another woman. I wasn't going to get into all of the gory details with my little sister.

"You should come," Suzette said. "Get your mind off things."

"You want me to hang out with a bunch of teenagers?" I asked, trying to put a teasing note into my voice and failing.

"Okay, old man, so we're a few years younger than you, but everyone other than me is legally an adult."

I smiled again. Suzette had graduated young from high school and had turned seventeen just last week, so I tended to forget her college friends were older than her.

"I don't know," I said.

"Come with us," she begged, that little girl pleading in her voice. "Once we're there, you can go do your own thing. Don't you think it'll be good to get out of the city for a while?"

"I'm already out of the city," I said. "I'm in Denver."

She let out a low whistle. "That must've been one hell of a break-up."

"You have no idea," I muttered.

"Then drive up and meet us. You'll have a car and can leave whenever you want."

She had a point, and what else was I going to do all weekend? Sit around the hotel and watch pay-per-view? Half of it would be porn and the last thing

15

I wanted to see right now were titles for lesbians going at it. Plus, we always kept extra clothes at the cabin, which meant I wouldn't need to spend the weekend in either my dirty clothes or a towel.

"All right," I agreed. If nothing else, I could count on a bunch of college kids having beer which meant I could sleep and drink my way through the next couple days.

That sounded as good a plan as any.

Chapter 2

Cabin might not be the most accurate word for the place my dad owned in Vail, Colorado. It wasn't right in Vail, but further up in the mountains. Close enough to get to when we wanted something, but far enough away that we needed to use a car or snowmobile to get there. We owned several acres of woods, including a few private ski runs Dad had made when he'd first bought the place. As for the building itself, it was two stories with five bedrooms on each floor. There was also a kitchen and living room on the first floor. While the rooms weren't large, they were big enough that sharing wasn't a big deal. While we called it a cabin, it was actually a decent-sized house.

When I pulled up to the house, I was glad it was so big. Suzette had said she was bringing some friends, I'd thought one or two. She'd brought six. I recognized Matt, Suzette's boyfriend. I thought he was kind of a douche, but at least he wasn't a total jackass like the last one.

The petite brunette next to Suzette was Abby, her roommate. I'd met her once when I'd visited Suzette on campus. She was sweet and quiet, balancing my talkative and sometimes too-blunt sister.

"Rylan!" Suzette threw herself in my arms as soon as I got out of the car. I hugged her back, really glad to see her. Our parents weren't exactly affectionate, but Suzette more than made up for it.

"Hey, Suze." I ruffled her hair. It was the same dark brown as mine, but our eyes were different colors. Hers were hazel like her mother's. Mine were blue-violet. Still, people told us we looked alike.

"I'm so glad you came." She linked her arm through mine and pulled me across the snow toward the group of people who were still standing next to a pair of cars. "Inside for introductions!"

I smiled as everyone moved to obey. My sister may have been the youngest of the group, but it was clear who was the dominating force. Yet another thing we had in common.

"Where's your luggage?" she asked as she picked up her bag from the back of her car.

"Don't have any." I patted my laptop. "This is pretty much all I walked out of the apartment with."

Her eyes grew wide. "Wow. You weren't kidding. You wanna talk about it?"

"Absolutely not," I said. "I don't want to think about it at all."

To my surprise, she grinned at me. "I was hoping you'd say that."

18

I gave her a puzzled look, but she didn't explain. I didn't ask. She'd share soon enough.

When we stepped into the living room, pounding the snow from our boots, the rest of the group was already there.

"Rylan, you know Matt and Abby."

I nodded at them both and they nodded back.

"That's Don." She pointed toward the other guy. He was easily three or four inches taller than me, which was saying something. But despite his bulk, the way he looked at Abby told me he was more of a teddy bear than a grizzly. "He's Abby's boyfriend. Pre-med."

"Nice to meet you." I raised my hand in greeting before the next person spoke.

"I'm Denise, Don's cousin." She was taller than Suzette, putting her at nearly six feet, but where my sister was slender, Denise had some serious curves. Her light brown hair was pulled back in a ponytail and the look in her dark eyes was one I'd seen many times before.

"And those two are Misty and Kristy," Suzette said. "They're my and Abby's suite-mates."

Misty and Kristy were identical from their strawberry blond curls to their bright green eyes. As I looked at the winter coats covering what appeared to be petite figures, I couldn't help but wonder if they were identical *all* over.

"Suzette's told us all about her big brother." One of the twins – Misty, I thought – ran her eyes over me and I knew I wasn't mistaking the innuendo.

19

"Nice of you to join us," Kristy said equally flirtatious.

"Let's get settled in," Suzette said, a big grin on her face. "Matt and I are taking my room."

She glanced at me and I shrugged. She was past the age of consent and her parents knew she was coming here with her boyfriend. They weren't stupid enough to think they wouldn't be sharing a room. If they didn't care, it wasn't any of my business.

"Mine's on the first floor," I said. "Break up the upstairs however you want, but make sure whoever's in the main room on the second floor doesn't mess it up."

"Our dad's really particular," Suzette explained. She grinned at Abby and Don. "Probably shouldn't put you two in there. If you break the bed, Dad will be seriously pissed."

"Suze!" Abby flushed, but she didn't look entirely displeased with the thought.

"And on that note," I said and started for the hallway. As I heard Suzette handing out the rest of the room assignments, I could feel eyes on me as I walked away. I wondered if it was the twins or Denise. I wasn't about to act on anything, not with my sister's friends, but after Lara's rejection, the admiration didn't exactly hurt my ego.

I put my laptop on the table next to my bed and went to my closet. I quickly changed out of the dress clothes I'd been wearing and into a pair of jeans and a sweatshirt.

"Ry." Suzette knocked on the door.

"Come in." I tossed my dirty clothes into a basket.

She opened the door, but didn't come in. She leaned against the doorframe, her expression serious. "I know you said you don't want to talk about it—"

"And I don't." My tone was mild, but I hoped she'd get the message.

"That's why I think it was so good you came with us." She glanced over her shoulder. "Denise and the twins, they think you're hot."

I rolled my eyes. "Seriously, Suze?"

She held up her hands in a gesture of surrender. "Hear me out."

Knowing her, I didn't have much of a choice, so I decided not to waste my time arguing. I twirled my finger for her to continue.

"They're not looking for a relationship, and I'm pretty sure they wouldn't mind helping you get over yours."

"Didn't you once tell me that if you caught me hooking up with any of your friends you'd castrate me?" I reminded her with a smile.

"I may have said that." She grinned. "But this is different."

"How so?"

"Because I said that when I didn't want you seducing some poor innocent girl and then not call her the next day."

"Would I do that?" I asked, all innocence.

She raised an eyebrow. "Do you really want me

21

to answer that?"

I laughed.

"I know that's not you," she said, her tone sobering. "But I didn't want to have to deal with the heartbreak if someone misunderstood your intentions." She jerked her head back toward the living room. "But those three, they won't misunderstand because they're not looking for anything beyond a good time."

I sighed. "You might think that, Suze, but you'd be surprised how many women who say they don't want a relationship change their mind when it comes to money."

"You're probably going to be pissed, but the girls and I already talked about that."

"Excuse me?"

She held up a finger, telling me to wait. "When you said you'd come, I had a frank talk with my friends. Trust me on this. If you want to hook up with any of them this weekend, they'd be game and I don't mind." She winked at me. "Think of it as your own personal Vegas. What happens here, stays here."

I shook my head as she walked away. Sure, her friends were hot, but I wasn't going to act on what she'd said. I was here to forget about the shit storm my love life had become. Drink, sleep, maybe ski.

First, drink.

I waited until I heard Suze and her friends head out to ski before I left my room. A couple of beers sounded pretty good right about now. In fact, I wouldn't have said no to something a bit stronger.

Chapter 3

I didn't actually get drunk, not slurring my words, staggering around, black-out drunk anyway. I was one of those guys who was always too responsible to get completely hammered because I was worried about doing something stupid. Even now, when all I wanted to do was forget, I couldn't bring myself to drink that much. Instead, I sat in front of the fireplace and watched the flames flicker as I nursed first one and then the second bottle of beer.

The alcohol took the edge off at least, making things fuzzy and seem a lot less important. Thinking about Lara didn't hurt anymore, not really. It was more of a dull ache rather than a sharp pain. The anger toward her for cheating and lying had faded as well. Unfortunately, with its departure it left room for me to be depressed.

The future yawned open in front of me, dark and empty. All of the plans I'd had were gone. No house.

What was point, after all? I'd wanted to buy that big, beautiful house for a family I was never going to have. I'd lost the woman I'd thought I was going to spend the rest of my life with. The woman I was going to marry, who was going to be the mother of my children. When this weekend was over, I was going back to my nice, empty apartment and my lucrative business and have no future aside from the money I could make.

The problem was, I didn't care about money, not really. I enjoyed the things I could do and buy, but what I really wanted was someone to share all of this with.

I glared at my now-empty beer bottle as if it was the reason I was slumped here on the couch feeling sorry for myself. I stood up and made my way back to the kitchen. I tossed my bottle into the recycling bin and stood at the refrigerator for a few minutes, trying to decide if I wanted to try some food or another drink. Suzette and her friends had brought a ton of junk food, the kind I remembered thriving on in college.

I grabbed a bag of munchies and headed back to my room. I didn't want to drink anymore and I didn't want to be here when the others came back from skiing and hiking. I wasn't exactly trying to avoid them, but I was pretty sure I wouldn't be very good company at the moment. No need to ruin their vacation.

What I really needed was to relax and then sleep off the rest of the day. I glanced outside. The sun was starting to set, which meant they'd be back soon. I headed into the bathroom and when I was finished, I made a decision. Relax. The hot tub sounded really good at the moment.

My dad and step-mom had wanted something small and intimate, but Suzette and I had convinced them to get one big enough that half a dozen people could be seated in comfort. As I headed for the enclosed back porch where they'd installed the tub, I wished they'd gotten the smaller one. I didn't want any chance of company.

The area was empty when I arrived, so I set my towel on the bench in front of the fireplace and pushed the button to start a fire. The air in here was chilly and I set the flame on low, just wanting to take the edge off. The real heat would come from the water.

It didn't take the tub long to heat up and I sighed when I stepped in. I took my favorite place, right where a couple jets would pound into my muscles like an amazing massage. I leaned my head back and closed my eyes and the water kneaded the sore muscles. It was heaven, exactly what I needed.

I must've dozed because the next thing I knew, a noise startled me awake. I opened my eyes and it took my brain a minute to figure out what I was seeing.

Denise stood at the edge of the tub wearing a slinky silk robe that showed off the curves I'd admired before. She smiled down at me and untied the belt. I swallowed hard and sat up straight.

"I thought you could use a little company." She let the robe fall.

Fuck.

Large, firm breasts that were gorgeous but just imperfect enough for me to know they were real. Hips that offered something to hold on to. Her pussy was neatly trimmed and her nipples were already starting to harden. She held up her hand and, between her fingers, was a condom.

"Denise." I shifted uncomfortably. My cock was starting to harden just from looking at her, but I was trying very hard not to listen to it. "I don't think this is a good idea."

"I think it is." She stepped into the water and made her way toward me, her breasts swaying a hypnotic invitation. She stopped right in front of me and leaned over. Her breasts moved tantalizingly close to my face as she set the condom down on the edge of the hot tub.

I closed my eyes. I wasn't going to give in. I felt hands on my thighs, tugging at my shorts and opened my eyes. Denise was kneeling in front of me, the water around her shoulders.

"Just sit back and enjoy the ride."

Before I could protest, she ducked under the water and, a moment later, I felt her mouth around my cock.

"Shit!" My hands opened and closed as she took all of my cock into her mouth. I was only half-hard, but as her tongue and lips went to work, she had to let more of me slip out. After longer than I'd have thought possible, she came up for air.

"I'm on the CSU swim team." She smiled at me as she moved to straddle my lap. She rubbed against my cock, her hands in my hair, her breasts pressed into my chest.

Dammit. I was no saint.

I grabbed the back of her neck and pulled her toward me. My lips crashed into hers with bruising force and I thrust my tongue into her mouth, tasting the chlorine from the water and my own flavor. Her hands ran over my chest and across my nipples. She broke the kiss and made her way down my throat and across my chest, licking and sucking at my sweat-slicked skin. When her teeth scraped across my nipple, I moaned. I grabbed her hips.

"Stand up."

She stood on the seat and I wrapped my arms around her legs to keep her steady even as I pressed my mouth against her pussy. Her fingers dug into my hair, pressing my face closer. I thrust my tongue between her folds, lapping at the moisture I found there. Her clit was already hard and throbbing, and she cried out as I wrapped my lips around it. I felt her muscles beginning to shake.

Damn she had a quick trigger. I thrust two fingers into her and she came.

She tugged at my hair, almost making my eyes water, but I kept working over her clit with my tongue and pumping my fingers in and out. I twisted them, rubbing my knuckles against her g-spot until her entire body was convulsing. Only then did I stop.

I stood, wrapping my arms around her and lifting her out of the tub. She was almost too tall, but I managed to get her onto her back without too much trouble. As I settled between her legs, I picked up the condom wrapper and tore it open. I looked down at Denise when I smelled blueberries.

"I like blueberries." She grinned up at me and licked her lips. "I want you to finish in my mouth."

I wasn't going to say no to that. I rolled the condom over my shaft and stroked myself a couple times. Maybe I did just need to lose myself in a woman.

"Let's see if you fuck with your cock as well as you do with your mouth."

I raised an eyebrow and she laughed. "Come on, Rylan, smile. You're far too serious."

I smiled as I reached down and hooked her legs over my arms. "You want me to fuck you?"

She nodded.

"How hard?" I leaned forward and buried myself inside her in one thrust.

She wailed, her back arching. I pulled back and then surged forward, making her cry out again.

"How hard do you want it?" I asked. I moved faster, driving deep, taking her hard.

"Harder," she gasped out. She grabbed my ass, nails digging into my skin as she urged me on.

I bent my head, sucking on one of her nipples as I fucked her. She was a loud and enthusiastic lover, writhing beneath me, her pussy contracting around my cock. She came twice while I was inside her, each time screaming so loudly I was sure everyone in the house would hear.

I felt my balls tightening, the pressure inside me growing. I pulled back and she made a sound of protest. Her legs splayed to either side, her hand automatically moving to take my place. Three fingers slid into her pussy and she ran out her tongue to lick her lips. She crooked a finger at me and made a 'come hither' motion.

"In my mouth." I didn't need the reminder.

I pulled off the condom and tossed it aside. Even as she started working herself toward another climax, I moved up her body, straddling her shoulders. I leaned forward and her lips parted. Placing my hands on the floor, I began to thrust into her hot, wet mouth. I kept the strokes shallow, but when she began to suck, I knew I wasn't going to last much longer.

Her tongue teased at the tip and then I felt a hand on my ass, pushing me deeper, more urgently. I let her take me as far as she wanted. I swore as she took me into her throat. When she swallowed, that was it. My eyes squeezed closed as I came.

I straightened, leaving a trail of cum across her lips as my softening cock slid out of her mouth. She licked it clean, even as her body shuddered with another climax. I moved off her to sit on the bench for a moment. She rolled onto her side, her fingers playing with her nipple.

"You're even better than I imagined."

I raised an eyebrow as I reached for my towel

and began to dry myself off. "Thought about it a lot, have you?"

"I knew who you were," she admitted. "And I'd heard some stories."

"Really?" I had to admit, I was mildly curious.

She shrugged. "I go to some clubs where your name's mentioned. I just wanted to see what all the fuss was about."

"And?" I was surprised. Lara was the only person I'd been with for the past two years. I wouldn't have thought anyone I'd been with before would've still been talking about me.

"The hype doesn't do you justice." She stood and walked over to where she'd left her robe. "And don't worry," she said. "I'm not after anything. Just wanted a good lay, and you were definitely that."

I watched as she left and wondered if she was telling the truth. I certainly hoped so, because things would be awkward for the rest of the weekend if she wasn't. I waited to give her the time necessary to get to her room and then I headed for mine. As dumb as my actions may have been, they did do one good thing. I felt relaxed and my mind cleared. Maybe I'd actually be able to sleep tonight.

Chapter 4

I managed to sleep for nearly seven solid hours, no dreams, no disturbances. The closest I came to a disturbance was when I finally woke, pulled out of my sleep by the squeaking of bed springs and the unmistakable sounds of two people fucking.

I lay there, still half asleep, and hoped I was hearing Abby and Don because I really didn't want my sister to be the one making all of that noise. I knew she was having sex with her boyfriend, but knowing it and hearing it were two completely different things.

I got up and headed for the bathroom before any of the others remembered there was one down here too. By the time I got out, I heard them all in the kitchen, laughing and talking. Then I smelled bacon and smiled. Suzette may have grown up in a house where a cook made most of the meals, but she'd always been in the kitchen, wanting to help. Of all the things people found surprising about my sister, her ability to cook was usually near the top of the list.

When I headed into the kitchen, part of me was worried that Denise would be there, acting weird or clingy. As much as I'd enjoyed the sex, I was starting to regret it. A couple minutes of pleasure – well, more than a couple – wouldn't be worth a weekend of fending off advances or explaining to Denise why last night had been a one-time thing. Or, worse, having to tell Suzette why her friend was pissed at me.

"Morning!" Suzette called from where she stood at the stove. She waved the spatula at me. "There's bacon, pancakes and scrambled eggs over on the counter." She made a face. "And Matt made some sort of kale smoothie thing if you'd prefer that."

"I'm training for the Boston Marathon," he told me as he leaned against the counter and stared at my sister's ass.

"We're all going to go cheer him on," Abby said. "You should totally come with us."

"Knowing my workaholic brother, he'll have some software emergency." Suzette grinned at me. "He's just a big computer geek, after all, preferring to spend his time in front of screen rather than with real people."

With all of the affection a big brother could muster, I flipped her off. She laughed and returned the gesture.

"There's like, what, six years between the two of you?" Misty asked from where she sat at the table, nibbling on a piece of bacon. I knew it was her because I could see the 'M' charm on her necklace.

"Six and a half," Suzette answered. "But he didn't come to live with our dad until he was older."

"I'm surprised you're so close," Don spoke up. "I have a step-brother who's five years younger than me and we pretty much see each other at holidays and only sometimes."

I shrugged. "You know how it is with Suze. She gets her way."

"I do," she agreed. "And I decided that I wanted my big brother around. Lucky for him, I let him stay."

It was time to steer the discussion away from me before anyone could ask even more personal questions. Like why I'd agreed to come this weekend or what I'd been doing last night.

"What are the plans for today?" I piled food on my plate and headed over to the table. As I passed Denise, I risked a glance. She smiled at me, but it wasn't anything more or less special than it had been yesterday. If anything, there was less to it than there had been before. Friendly, but the lust was more tempered.

"We're all going to head over to the Vail Ski Resort," Kristy said as she sat down next to me. "You're coming, right?"

"We have perfectly good trails here to ski on," I said as I reached for the maple syrup.

"We're not going for just the trails," Abby said. "There's shopping and food." She looked over at Suzette. "No offense meant to your cooking."

"None taken," Suzette said cheerfully. "I'm not going to say no to dinner in a nice restaurant." She shot Matt a meaningful look.

"Got the hint the first time, babe." He sounded more amused than annoyed, and my estimation of him went up.

"I think I'll take a rain check," I said.

"What did I say?" Suzette brought over her own plate and sat down across from me. "Anti-social."

"Fine," I said. "You want me to be social, I'll be social." I stabbed a pancake more viciously than it deserved and glared at her.

"Like you said, I get what I want." Suzette grinned as she poured liberal amounts of syrup on her pancakes.

"Yeah, yeah," I mumbled. I knew what she was trying to do. She assumed that if I stayed around here for the second day in a row, I would spend the entire time moping about Lara. The fact that she was probably right annoyed me to no end.

I insisted on driving separately so I could leave if I wanted to, but my trip to the resort wasn't a peaceful one. Suzette climbed into my car with a wide smile that told me I was going to spend the entire drive having a conversation with my sister I didn't want to have.

"So," she said as we started down the mountain. "You banged Denise last night."

"Really?" I gave her as mean a look as I dared while paying attention to the road. "That's what you want to talk about?" I sighed. "When did she tell

36

you?"

"She didn't. Well, not exactly anyway. Last night, I knew you were in the hot tub and she said she was going to check it out. She was gone for about a half hour and, this morning, the both of you looked very relaxed." Suzette's eyes were dancing as she teased me. "I knew you couldn't resist."

"Kinda hard when she's got her mouth around my cock," I muttered, annoyed.

"She's on the swim team," Suzette said, managing to say it with a straight face.

"She mentioned that," I said dryly.

"Underwater blow-jobs are kind of her claim to fame around the campus."

I glanced at my sister. "And this is the same school I went to?" I shook my head. "A lot's changed in four years."

"Not from what I've heard," she replied. "You were just a geek."

"Thanks."

"A hot one, based on pretty much every straight woman or gay man I've talked to, but still a geek."

"You know," I said. "I've really missed these heart-to-heart talks."

She laughed at my sarcastic tone. "You know you love me."

I sighed. "I do." She was right. I loved my parents, but the majority of it was obligatory. There were only two people in my life who had never let me down, had never done anything to make me question where I stood with them.

37

One was Zeke Wesson, my best friend growing up. He'd been there for me through all of the crap with my mom and had been the one who'd protected me from bullies before I hit my growth spurt sophomore year. He'd been the popular kid, a jock and someone all the girls had loved. In school, I'd always been an outsider and he'd made sure I never completely drifted away. In return, I'd offered him solace from a shitty home life. He was the closest thing to a brother I had.

The other person, of course, was Suzette. Our age difference didn't matter, and neither of us cared that we only shared one biological parent. She was my sister and I'd do anything to protect her. She was the same way. We looked out for each other, even after I'd moved out to go to school. It was always the two of us against our parents and against the world. Now that Suzette was getting older, I wondered if she and Zeke might end up together. I could honestly say I liked the idea. Some guys wouldn't want their best friend with their sister, but I thought it would be nice to have him be more of a part of the family and there wasn't anyone I would trust more with my sister.

"Earth to Rylan." Suzette poked my arm.

"Ow." I glared at her. "What was that for?"

"I kept saying your name and you weren't answering." Her eyes narrowed. "You weren't thinking about Lara were you?"

"No," I answered honestly. "Just thinking about how you and Zeke are the only two people I could count on." I glanced over at her as I followed Matt and Don into the parking lot. "You two get along, right?"

"Sure, I guess." She shrugged. "But I don't want to talk about your best friend. I want to talk about you and how you're doing."

"I'm fine," I said, pulling into a parking space.

"You're fine as in you got laid last night so things aren't looking quite so bad? Or fine as in I'm lying to you because I don't want you to see how hurt I am?"

I glared at her. "How about fine as in I don't want to talk about my break-up or my sex life with my little sister?"

She held up her hands in the universal sign for surrender. "Okay, okay, I get it. I won't ask about it again." As she climbed out of the car, she added, "But if you're still that grumpy, maybe you need to get laid again."

I opened my mouth to say something smart, but she'd already closed the door and was heading over to where the others had parked. I scowled. I loved her, but sometimes I wanted to throttle her. Family. Go figure. I sighed and climbed out of the car before she could start sharing her observations with her friends regarding my need for more sex.

As I got out of the car, I wondered if she was right. Once I'd gotten over the shock last night, I'd enjoyed myself. Denise had been enthusiastic and not shy about telling me what she'd wanted. But it had just been straight sex, pretty vanilla stuff. Maybe what I really needed was something more intense, something to let off a bit more steam.

I pushed the thought aside and forced a smile. It wasn't like I was going to do anything about it right now. Maybe some other kind of physical activity would get my mind off of things. I wasn't a jock or anything like that, I never had been, but I'd always been good at skiing and I enjoyed it. I may have had my fair share of flings in the past, but I wasn't one of those guys who used skiing as an excuse to pick up women. I liked the athleticism of it.

"So, what do you want to do first?" Misty asked, tossing her curls over her shoulder. "Cup of hot cocoa? Some shopping?"

I refrained from rolling my eyes. "I'm thinking a quick run down a fairly easy slope to warm up."

"Up for some company?" Kristy asked.

I looked over at Suzette who just smiled and waved as she and Matt headed for one of the stores. Abby and Don followed them. I glanced over to where I'd last seen Denise. If my sister had left me here with all three of her single friends, she and I were going to have a not-so-pleasant conversation.

Denise, however, had her sights set on a pair of college-aged guys who were standing at the ski rental and checking her out. Apparently, Suzette had been right. Unless Denise was trying to make me jealous, she really didn't seem to care about last night.

"Well," Misty said, linking her arm through mine. "What do you say you come with us to rent some skis and then we'll take a couple passes together?"

I gently disentangled my arm from hers. I wanted some time to myself, but I didn't want to be rude. The girls were a bit forward... okay, a lot forward, but they were nice enough and they were Suze's friends. I wasn't going to be a jerk to them for something like this.

"How about you two catch up to me when you can." I smiled at them both and hurried away before they could say anything else. A quick glance over my shoulder said they weren't following and they also didn't look pissed, so that was even better.

When I reached the top, I breathed a sigh of relief. The air was sharp and cold, breaking through the haze that had been surrounding me. I'd chosen one of the medium slopes to get my legs under me again and I took it easy on the way down. It had been a couple years since I'd skied and I was pleasantly surprised at how quickly it came back.

It didn't take me long to work my way back up to the more difficult slopes and I found myself enjoying the way the journey down helped clear my mind. I was able to focus on one thing at a time, letting my body move on instinct and muscle memory while my mind focused only on the next obstacle in front of me.

I didn't know how long it would last, but I was going to take advantage of it for as long as I could.

Chapter 5

Four hours. That's how long I was able to keep myself from thinking about Lara and everything that had happened. Four glorious hours without anything in my head beyond the next turn of my skis or the tilt of my body. I didn't speak to anyone and no one spoke to me. I saw a couple women looking my way and a few guys too, but I kept my eyes on where I was headed and left it at that.

I caught a glimpse of the others periodically as they took the easier trails, but I didn't approach them. I waved when one of them waved, but that was about it. As noon passed, though, I started to get hungry and knew I couldn't keep going without something in my stomach. Stopping, however, meant thinking again. I made my way back to the main lodge and ordered something to eat. By the time the food came, depression was already descending.

I'd have to deal with it sooner or later, work through all those stages. Anger, denial, and the rest.

I'd have to admit that things weren't going to be the same as they had been for the past few years. I'd have to start making new plans.

But not today.

I ate in sullen silence, unable to get the thought of Lara out of my mine. Suzette's previous statement about needing to get laid again and my own thoughts about the nature of my encounter with Denise all mixed and memories began to flash through my mind.

Lara's jade eyes glittered up at me. "Make sure you tie me up tight. I almost got free last time."

I tightened the knots around her ankles and her wrists, bending and contorting her body into a position that left her wide open and vulnerable. Most of the women I'd been with before had liked handcuffs or the occasional scarf. Not Lara. She wanted me to use rope to completely immobilize her.

Once I was sure she wasn't going to get free, I went down on her, licking and sucking until she came. After the first, I added fingers, thrusting two into her hot, wet pussy without warning. She cried out and then writhed on my fingers as I pumped them into her. I licked and sucked every inch of her soft, delicious flesh, reveling in the sounds of her moans and cries. I made her come over and over again until she begged me to stop. But I didn't. I kept going until she finally said her safe word. Only then did I grant her respite.

I closed my eyes. Fuck. I didn't want to think

about that. I was already tense enough. I didn't need those memories to make things worse. It was too late though. No amount of skiing would clear my head now. In fact, if I was stupid enough to try to get on the slopes again, I'd probably ski myself into a tree and subsequent coma.

I needed a new distraction away from this place. Get some work done. That would keep me from thinking about Lara.

I waited until I was already in my car before I texted Suzette and told her I was heading back to the cabin. I figured that way, she couldn't try to talk me out of it. I wouldn't answer the phone or text while I was driving and she wouldn't be able to get to the parking lot before I pulled out.

When I arrived at the cabin, I had three texts and a voicemail. She didn't sound angry, but she didn't sound entirely pleased with me either. The one thing I could tell, however, was that she was concerned. I shot her back another text letting her know I was okay and that I just needed to get some work done.

It wasn't entirely a lie. Okay didn't mean good, and considering what had happened, I thought I was doing okay. And I was planning on doing some work.

I brought my laptop into the living room, started a fire and tried to lose myself in the numbers and safety of coding. Instead, I found myself drawn back into memories.

Lara was bent over the edge of the couch, her

body quivering from the aftermath of an orgasm so intense that she'd almost passed out. Now, I was about to begin again. I twisted my wrist and the thin strips of leather cracked in the air. This was her favorite flogger. It offered just enough pain to turn her on and the handle had been specially made to double as a dildo. I'd used it on her earlier and it was still slick with her juices. I tightened my grip and brought the leather down on her ass. My cock hardened as she whimpered.

I shook my head. Not again. No more thinking. I shifted in my seat. My cock didn't agree with my sentiment. It liked the idea of thinking about Lara and enjoying a bit of alone time.

My hand stung but not as much as her ass had to. It was cherry red and she'd have a hell of time sitting for the next day or so, but her pussy was dripping wet.

"Dammit," I muttered. I'd been staring at this code for ten minutes and hadn't seen a thing.

"Harder, baby. Fuck me harder."

I pounded into her as she struggled against her restraints. She knew she couldn't get free, but she liked knowing it and testing it. I tugged on the chains connected to her nipple clamps and she cried out. They had to be sore – I'd been playing with them all night – but she didn't cry off. If anything, she came harder.

I put aside the laptop and sighed. There was no way I would to get work done like this. What pissed me off the most was that I wasn't even remembering all of the shitty stuff. It wasn't the memory of Lara being eaten out by our neighbor or any of the arguments we'd had over the past two years. It wasn't the times she'd driven me nuts or all of her annoying little habits.

No, of course not. I was getting surround-sound and technicolor replays of our sex life. Which, now that I thought about it, had been strangely satisfying considering she'd informed me she was a lesbian. Then again, for all I knew, she'd either faked her orgasms or had been pretending I was some leggy brunette. I was willing to bet the latter, because she'd been the one who'd wanted the kinkier shit. If she'd just been going through the motions sexually, she wouldn't have cared as much. Right?

I stood up and ran my hands through my hair. I walked over to the French doors and looked outside. It had started to snow. Lightly, so I didn't think it'd cause the others any problem getting back.

Maybe, I thought, I shouldn't be here when they returned. Maybe I should get out of here. I wouldn't be any fun for them to have around. They would probably play some games or something when they got back. Strip charades or some shit like that. A drinking game that would lead to the guys cheering for the girls to kiss. I didn't want to be involved in any of that, especially if one of those girls was my sister.

No, I knew what I needed and it wasn't here. I needed the release that came with dominating someone. I needed to be in control of something, needed to find some semblance of order in all of this. From the first moment I'd been introduced to the BDSM lifestyle, I'd felt something inside me click. It didn't get me off because I felt some chauvinistic right to take what I wanted. Part of the control aspect was trust, and that appealed to me. Even if it was only a one time hook up, they still had to trust me.

And that was what Lara had broken.

My eyes burned and I started to feel the pain that came with the end of a two year relationship.

I needed to get out of here. Needed to find a real release. It wasn't a very long ride back to Denver. I could get there just as the clubs were starting to fill up. I could watch a scene or two, find a willing Sub and fuck the hell out of her. Tie her up. Spank her. Do some of those things I'd remembered doing with Lara.

I closed my eyes. That wouldn't make me feel better, no matter how much my cock was interested in pursuing that idea. I didn't want to deal with the hassle of finding a Sub and setting up those rules. I hadn't had to do that since Lara and I had gotten together and I didn't think I'd be able to handle going through all of that. It wouldn't be about me forgetting, but rather a reminder of what I'd lost.

Alcohol and sleep it was then.

But, first, I wanted a shower. I'd been sitting long enough that my muscles had started to stiffen. I tried to stay in shape and work out, but it had been a while since I'd spent that many hours doing that much activity. A hot shower to soothe my muscles would be a good way to relax before finding something to drink and spending the rest of the night in my room.

The sound of the water was enough white noise to keep most of the memories at bay and it was tempting to stay in until I used up all the hot water. I didn't do it, but the bathroom was still full of steam by the time I got out. I quickly toweled off and wrapped the towel around my waist. I wasn't sure if the others were back yet, but my room was just across the hall from the bathroom and I didn't think it'd bother anyone if I crossed those couple feet in a towel that covered everything important.

I heard them in the living room when I opened the bathroom door, but no one seemed to be close or looking for me, so I walked across the hall and into my room. I shut the door behind me and tossed my towel toward the basket I used for dirty clothes. It wasn't until I turned around that I realized I wasn't alone.

Chapter 6

"We thought you might want some company since you spent all day alone on the slopes."

Misty was still wearing her 'M' necklace, but judging by the bare shoulders, I was willing to bet she wasn't wearing anything else. Kristy was equally naked, I assumed, save for her 'K' necklace.

"What are you two doing?" I tried to make myself sound like the stern older brother, but I wasn't quite sure it was working since they both looked more amused than abashed.

"Come on, Rylan," Kristy spoke this time. "We're all adults here."

I raised an eyebrow.

"We turned twenty last week," Misty said.

Shit, they were the same age as Lara. I couldn't use age as an excuse as to why this was a very bad idea.

And I suddenly realized I was naked. I started to reach for my towel and stopped when the twins smirked. I hadn't done anything wrong, and I didn't have anything to be ashamed of. Fuck it. Let them stare. Like they said. They were both adults.

"Look, you're Suzette's friends," I said, crossing my arms over my chest.

"Didn't stop you from fucking Denise." Kristy grinned.

I scowled.

"Relax, she didn't kiss and tell," Misty said. "We agreed that she should go first and, well, the two of you weren't exactly quiet."

"You agreed what?" I was starting to rethink the whole no-pants thing.

"Well, Suzette mentioned you might need some cheering up this weekend and she knew that the three of us are always looking for a good fuck," Kristy said.

I was going to kill my sister.

Misty continued, "We talked and agreed that Denise should go first."

"And why was that?" I took a step toward the bed, curious despite myself.

"Because Misty and I can be a lot to handle and we weren't sure you'd be up for it." Kristy winked. She pushed herself up enough that the blanket slipped halfway down her breasts.

I looked from one to the other. My brain insisted this was a bad idea, even worse than having fucked Denise. That was one of my sister's friends. This was two. Sisters. And they were Suzette's suite-mates. It was a recipe for something beyond disaster.

"No string attached, Rylan. We don't do

relationships." Misty's hand disappeared beneath the blanket. She moaned, making a pleased sound and I wondered exactly what her hand was doing under there.

My cock gave an interested twitch. I'd managed to make it behave by telling myself not to be stupid. There was no way I could stop it from reacting to the noises Misty was making and the mental images my brain insisted on creating.

"What my sister and I do, however, is fuck." Kristy tossed off the blanket, revealing a petite body with small but firm breasts and a smooth pussy. "We share guys all the time, so there's no need to be shy."

"And don't even think about being gentle," Misty added.

More blood rushed to my cock.

Kristy got up on all fours as Misty uncovered herself. One look told me that the girls were indeed identical all over. I wondered if they'd feel the same wrapped around me, beneath me.

"We're not into vanilla," Misty said as she slid her fingers into her pussy.

Fuck. I really hoped she meant what I thought she meant.

"And we brought toys." Kristy climbed off the bed and picked up a bag I hadn't even seen. She opened it and pulled out a dildo that was almost as big as my cock. She kept her eyes on me as she handed the toy to her sister. "We're both into S&M, but our tastes vary a bit." She reached into the bag again and pulled out a flogger.

Okay, maybe I wouldn't kill my sister. At the moment, I thought buying her something expensive would be more appropriate.

"I'm first," Kristy said as she handed me the flogger. She looked up at me from under her lashes. "Our safe word is always Gemini."

I raised an eyebrow and she smiled.

"You have any condoms in that bag of yours?" I asked.

Her smile widened and she pulled out a string of them, tossing them onto the bed. "Twenty bucks says you wear out before we do."

I flicked my wrist and cracked the flogger, watching as Kristy's bright green eyes darkened with lust. Without me saying a word, she went to her knees, hands clasped behind her back, head bowed. Oh, yeah, the girl was definitely a Sub.

"Are you doubting my stamina?" It was easier than I'd anticipated, falling into the Dominant role.

"No, Sir." Her eyes flicked up and then back down again. "Or do you prefer Master?"

Damn. She'd been trained by someone who knew what they were doing. My stomach tightened as I thought of all the other things her trainer and previous masters might've taught her.

"Sir," I said. I'd never really been a fan of the whole 'slave / master' terminology. "And I think you were doubting me." I cracked the flogger again and hoped that no one upstairs could hear it. Then I remembered what Misty had said about hearing Denise and me. For a second, I actually considered stopping. Then I remembered hearing one of the couples going at it this morning. Time for a little payback.

I closed the distance between Kristy and I until I could reach out and run the soft leather strips along the side of her face. I used the flogger to lift her chin until she was looking at me. Watching for even the slightest hint of negativity, I wrapped my free hand in her hair. If anything, the arousal in her eyes grew.

"Do you like that?" I asked. I tightened my grip until I knew I was pulling her hair.

"Yes, Sir," she gasped.

"Open your mouth," I said. "And keep your hands behind your back."

"Yes, Sir," she answered immediately. She opened her mouth, not overly wide like some women did to take someone large, but rather just enough so that I could push my way inside without hurting either of us.

I was more than half-hard as the tip of my cock passed between her lips. I groaned at the wet heat surrounded me as I slid deeper inside. I felt her start to gag as I neared the back of her mouth and pulled back, giving her the chance to cry off.

"I'm going to fuck your mouth," I said and brushed the leather strips across her breasts, watching her pale pink nipples harden. "And then I'm going to punish you for your challenge."

"Yes, please, Sir." Her voice was breathless.

When the head of my cock nudged her lips, she opened her mouth again and I slid inside. I started slow, using the first few strokes to gauge just how far I could push her. When she moaned, the vibration went straight through me and I went from mostly hard to fully erect. I knew I was too big for her to take all of me, but I was going to get as much as I could.

I held onto her hair to keep her head in place as I began to rock my hips. Her tongue moved around my cock as best it could, and then she began to suck, her cheeks hollowing out each time I pulled back. Whoever taught this girl to give a blow job deserved a pat on the back.

I pulled her toward me as I pushed forward, driving myself deeper than I had been, almost enough to make her gag, but not quite. I held her there for a few seconds, then released her, falling from her mouth with an obscene sound. She coughed a bit and was breathing heavily, but her eyes were shining.

"Stand up," I ordered.

She did, assuming the normal Sub position of head down, hands behind the back.

"Come toward me."

I moved back so that she'd have room. I held up a hand for her to stop when she was far enough from the bed that I could circle her. I'd seen her reaction when I'd touched her breasts with the flogger. I wasn't going to just whip her ass. She was going to get it all over.

"I'm going to use this." I cracked the flogger for emphasis. "On your ass. On your tits." She shivered.

I paused, and then added, "And on your cunt."

I heard her catch her breath, but there was no mistaking the flush of arousal. Part of the Dom's responsibility was to give the Sub the opportunity to use her safe word. Kristy had it now, but she wasn't taking it. Either she was willing to try something new or she already knew she liked what I was going to do. It didn't matter to me either way. Unless she said the word, it was going to happen.

I walked behind her. "Hands at your sides."

She obeyed instantly and I rewarded her with a swat across her ass. She gasped but didn't move. Pale pink lines appeared where the leather came in contact with her skin. I flicked my wrist again, catching her at a different angle. The sound she made hardened my cock even further. Yes. This was what I needed.

I circled around to the front of her and hit first one, then the other breast. I started easy, needing to see her reaction. She moaned as the stripes appeared on her pale flesh. Her nipples hardened into little bullet points. I began to circle her, alternating blows to her ass and breasts, always harder on her ass, but hard enough on her breasts. Her skin turned from pink to red as the leather hit the same places multiple times. Her cheeks were flushed and her mouth hung open, little sounds of pleasure escaping each time the flogger made contact.

"Can you come from this?" I asked, my tone conversational. "If I use this on your pussy, will you come?" I aimed at her nipple and she cried out at the contact.

"With your permission, Sir."

Damn she was good. "Spread your legs."

She moved her feet until they were shoulder-distance apart. I could see the moisture coating her pussy lips and along the insides of her thighs, leaving no doubt as to how much she enjoyed this. I ran the flogger between her legs, coating it with her juices. She whimpered, but didn't move.

"Come whenever you're ready," I said.

"Thank you, Sir."

I made the first blow light and she shuddered. I hadn't realized how close she already was. The second was harder and her body jerked in response. This one would do it, I knew. I swung as hard as I dared at such delicate flesh and the crack echoed in the room.

Kristy wailed, her knees buckling. She managed to catch herself, but I could see it was a struggle to stand as an orgasm ripped through her. I left her to recover as I picked up her bag of toys. Inside was a pair of nipple clamps. Metal with teeth and a chain connecting the two. I had a pretty good idea that these belonged to Kristy, but I didn't want to guess. For the first time since this had begun, I looked over at Misty.

She was on her back, working her fingers in and out of her pussy. As I watched, she picked up the dildo her sister had given her and used it to replace her fingers. She moaned, her eyelids fluttering as she fit the entire thing into her pussy. She opened her eyes then, the green nearly swallowed up in black. I held up the clamps and she gestured toward her sister.

I left Misty to her own devices and turned back to Kristy. I could still see small shivers going through her, but she was back in her Sub pose. I walked over to her and pinched one nipple between my forefinger and thumb. She made a small sound that became louder when I fastened the first clamp onto her. The second one made her entire body jerk. I gave the chain an experimental tug and watched her eyes roll back. Oh, she was definitely the M part of S&M.

I stuck my hand between her legs, my fingers slipping between her folds to find her as wet as I'd imagined she'd be. "You're soaking." I brushed my thumb across her swollen clit.

"Ah!" She shuddered.

I flicked my thumb back and forth rapidly, enjoying the way her body twitched, the way her emotions played across her face. She wanted to pull back, her flesh too sensitive, but at the same time, she couldn't help her body craving more friction, needing blessed release. Before she got there, however, I pulled my hand away.

"Sit on the edge." I gestured toward the bed.

I admired the deep red stripes across her ass as she crossed over to the bed and sat down. She winced, but didn't complain. I walked over to stand in front of her. My cock was rock hard, ready to go.

"Put one on me." I pointed at the condoms.

She opened one of the packets and rolled it over my cock, taking her time and stroking me until I moved her hand away.

"Lie back and pull your knees up." I reached out and hooked my finger around the chain. "But keep them off to the side." I gave the chain a little tug and she made a small sound in the back of her throat. "I'm going to play with those."

When she was spread open in front of me, I stepped up to the edge of the bed. I grabbed her hips, positioned myself at her dripping entrance and looked down at her.

"I'm going to fuck you hard," I said. "And I'm not going to let up until I come."

She spread her legs further apart.

I took that as an invitation and drove forward. Her back arched, her hands tightening on her thighs until her knuckles turned white. She yelled as I bottomed out, my balls bumping against her ass. She was wet enough there had been no resistance, but I was big and her body had to stretch to accommodate me. I didn't wait for it though. I pounded into her without pause. I felt her pussy start to spasm around me and knew she was close to coming again. I grabbed the chain connecting the nipple clamps and tugged.

"Fuck!" Kristy screamed, writhing on the bed, but never losing the grip on her legs. "More, please, Sir!"

I pulled again, leaning forward slightly so the

base of my cock rubbed against her clit. She screamed again and I had the presence of mind to clamp my hand down across her mouth.

"You're going to make everyone think I'm killing you." I heard the humor in my voice.

Kristy's cries were muffled now, but her body shook so hard that I had no doubt she was coming. Mine was close behind. I buried myself deep inside her, groaning as I came. I squeezed my eyes closed, losing myself in the pleasure of orgasm. As soon as I started to come down, however, I opened my eyes and pulled out. This wasn't about cuddling. I sat on the edge of the bed as Kristy let go of her legs, her limbs falling apart haphazardly. I reached over and carefully removed the clamps. She whimpered as they came off, her nipples left swollen and red. I leaned down and wrapped my lips around one of them.

"Shit!" she cried out as I sucked on the abused flesh. When I moved to the other one, she came again. Only then did I stop.

"Damn," Misty finally spoke.

I looked over at her.

"I really hope you're able to do that again." She removed the dildo from her pussy and got to her knees. "Well, not exactly that because that's not my particular kink, but you get the idea."

"What's your kink?" I raised an eyebrow.

She crawled across the bed, ignoring her still-panting sister. She reached down and pulled off the condom, tossing it into the nearby trash. She stretched out so that her head was in my lap and her tongue darted out, licking my sensitive shaft. I sucked in a breath. It was too soon after climax and the stimulation bordered on painful.

"If I'm naughty," she said, wiggling her ass. "I may need to be spanked." She licked me again.

I brought my hand down on her ass with a stinging slap. She moaned and moved her head lower, using one hand to cup my balls even as she licked them. I swore and smacked her ass again. My stomach clenched as Misty took my entire cock into her mouth. Blood rushed south, stiffening me again, but so fast it hurt. I grabbed her hair and lifted her off of me.

"My master may need to tie me up to make me behave." She grinned at me.

"So you're the saucy one." I tweaked one of her nipples and she yelped. I didn't mind a Sub who told me what she wanted. Sometimes, it was more freeing that way. I was in charge, but didn't have to worry about what to do. "And what should I do after I tie you up?"

"Whatever you want to do, Master."

"Sir." I slapped her ass hard enough to make my hand sting. "Not Master."

"Yes, Sir." There was a sing-song note to her voice.

Kristy finally regained enough strength to get up and crawl over to the spot Misty had vacated. She rolled onto her side, pulled the blankets over her and settled in to watch what came next.

I turned my attention back to the woman on my lap as Misty kissed her way up my chest, licking and sucking on my nipple. I buried my hand in her thick hair, giving myself a moment to enjoy the sensations of her teeth and tongue before pulling her off.

"Is there something in that bag of yours you want me to use?" I asked. "Handcuffs?"

She shook her head as best she could with the grip I had on her hair. I leaned down and picked up the bag, handing it to her. She reached in and pulled out a rope. An actual rope. She handed it to me.

"Tie me up, Sir. Please. Tie me up tight." She batted her lashes at me. "I'll be a very bad girl if you don't."

"Really?" My cock was definitely making a return. I'd learned all kinds of interesting ways to tie up a Sub and the thought of seeing Misty trussed up in any of those ways was turning me on. "Once I tie you up, what should I do with you?"

"Fuck me harder than you fucked my sister." She reached behind her and picked up the dildo she'd been using earlier. "And fuck my ass with this."

I smacked her ass and she cried out. "Are you telling me what to do?"

"No, Sir." She shook her head. "Never, Sir."

"So what should I do with you after I tie you up?" I repeated the question.

"Use me however you want, Sir. Any way that pleases you."

I got up and went to work with the rope. I tied her tightly, but used the kinds of knots that were easy to pull out of. Nothing spoiled the moment more than having to take the time after good sex to have to untie difficult knots. As I worked, I made sure to play with her nipples and tease her clit so that, by the time I was done, she was moaning and begging me to fuck her.

I'd left her on her knees, her arms bound behind her so that I could use them for leverage, but her chest pressed down so her ass was in the air. I picked up a condom and put it on. She'd done all the foreplay needed to keep her pussy loose and I could see now that her asshole glistened with what I assumed was lube.

"Did you prep your ass?" I asked her as I rubbed the head of my cock along her slit.

"Yes, Sir," Misty said, pushing back against me.

I smacked her ass. It was turning a nice shade of red. "I decide when I fuck you."

"Yes, Sir." She stopped moving.

I grabbed her hips and slammed into her. I went in much easier than I had with Kristy. As I thrust into Misty, I adjusted my grip, moving one hand to her bound wrists and the other so that I could work my thumb into her ass. It slipped in with little resistance and she moaned.

"More," she begged. "I need more."

I removed my thumb and smacked her ass cheek. She whimpered, her fingers flexing. I thought I knew what she wanted, but I needed to be sure. I didn't want to hurt her for real. I only liked inflicting pain if it gave pleasure. I wasn't a true sadist.

"Do you want me to fuck your ass now? Is that what you want?"

"Yes, please."

"You want me to shove this in your ass while I'm fucking you?" I picked up the toy.

"Yes, Sir. Please." Her skin was flushed.

I reached into the bag and felt around, quickly locating the lube I'd known would be there. I slicked the dildo quickly and then pressed the tip against her asshole. She moaned as I pushed the toy, inch by inch, inside. My cock was only partially inside, but I could feel her muscles spasming around the intrusion. She panted and moaned, but they were all sounds of pleasure so I kept going until the entire thing was buried in her ass.

I gave her a moment before I pulled it out and pushed it back in again. She cried out as I fucked her with the toy, each stroke rubbing against my cock through the thin skin between us and pushing me toward my own climax.

"Ready for the real fun?" I wrapped my hand around the rope between her wrists and held her as I shoved the dildo all the way inside. I held it in place and snapped my hips forward, driving myself as deep into her pussy as I could.

She wailed, her body convulsing around my cock. I squeezed my eyes shut, fighting for control. She was so fucking tight like this and her muscles were squeezing me even tighter. I had to stop for nearly a full minute before I could start moving again... fast, hard thrusts that made her scream my name every time. In the back of my head, I knew my sister would tease me about this for years, but I didn't care. I just needed to finish. I shifted my weight and began to drive her into the mattress, banging the headboard against the wall.

"Come," I growled the command. "Come!"

Her entire body tensed, every muscle tightening until it hurt. The pain drove me over the edge and I exploded. White hot pleasure poured through me, making me forget everything for several seconds of blissful ignorance. Dimly, I heard Misty swearing and then her body went limp under mine.

I pulled out and saw her twitch, as if she'd come again. I rolled off to the side, letting my pulse slow and my breathing relax. There was a creaking sound and I looked over to see Kristy pulling at the knots that held her sister. I pushed myself up and gently pulled the toy out of Misty's ass. She shuddered, but the look she gave me was pure lust. When she was finally untied, the girls stretched out on my bed and looked up at me expectantly.

I pulled off the condom and tossed it into the trash. I wasn't sure where things were going to go from here. Did I just send them back to their room? Their toys were laying around and I knew they had to be tired.

"That was amazing, Rylan," Kristy said. "I haven't had someone dominate me like that in a long time."

I nodded. "It was great."

Misty stretched and smiled up at me, a definite

66

cat-ate-the-canary grin. "Did we wear you out?"

I raised an eyebrow.

"The best thing about fucking twins," Misty said. "Is that there's always one ready to go." She looked at my cock. "You think you have a couple more rounds in you, or are you done for the night?"

"There you go again," I said. "Questioning my stamina." I grinned. I really did owe Suzette one.

Chapter 7

When I finally slept, it was solid and straight through. The girls had gone back to their room sometime in the early morning hours, both seeming like they still had energy to spare. As for me, I was exhausted. True to their word, the twins had worn me out. I'd come twice more – which I'd never done before – and I'd lost count of the number of time the girls orgasmed. There had been more toys in their bag and we'd used every one of them. When I climbed out of bed the next morning, I was actually sore and I knew not all of it was from skiing.

No one said anything to me as we packed up and got ready to head back home, but from the looks I got, everyone had definitely gotten an earful. Since no one acted annoyed, I didn't offer an apology. The only thing I'd been worried about was how the twins would behave, but they were just as cool about everything as Denise. I didn't know what kind of arrangements those three had, but I wasn't going to argue with it.

The only thing I was taking home with me was my dirty clothes, so I was ready to go before anyone else. As I put the basket in the back of my car, the twins and Denise came up to me.

"We just wanted to let you know that the three of us really enjoyed this weekend." Denise smiled at me, her eyes dancing.

"And if you're ever in the mood for another go, just look us up," Kristy said.

"A long weekend works too," Misty said. She winked at me. "Have a safe trip back and maybe we'll be seeing you around."

The trio walked off as Suzette approached. Judging by the gleam in her eyes, I was about to get an 'I told you so'.

"So..." She grinned at me. "Feeling better after your weekend away?"

I crossed my arms. "You know, little sister, you could always be the bigger person and not rub it in that you were right."

"I could," she admitted. "But it wouldn't be as much fun."

I sighed. "All right, I'll say it then. You were right. I needed some time to... get my mind off of things."

"And now?"

"Now?" I paused, thinking about everything that had happened over the past few days. "Now, I think I'm done with relationships."

"What?" She looked surprised.

"Hooking up with those girls this weekend,

seeing how easy it was for us to go our separate ways, it made me think that trying to find someone is pointless." I ran my hand through my hair. "I'm not going to go all forever bachelor or anything like that. I still want a family, eventually, and I'm still going to be open to falling in love, but I'm through with the whole dating scene. I'm just going to end up getting hurt, and until I find a woman who's worth that risk, I'm done."

Her face was blank as she gave me a hug and watched me get in the car. I wondered what she was thinking, but I wasn't going to ask. I wasn't sure I was ready to hear her thoughts. What I was ready to do was move on with my life. The first step was to get out of the apartment I'd shared with Lara. I didn't need to be with her to buy the house I loved. It had plenty of room for me to play until I found someone worth sharing my life with.

If I ever found her.

The End —

More Pleasure

Prologue

Her body was limp in my arms as I maneuvered us under the blankets. My muscles still trembled from how hard I'd come, but I managed to get us situated and comfortable. I slid my arms around her and pulled her close as she curled up against me, her head on my chest. The gesture looked so natural for her that it made my heart hurt. I stroked her dark hair as her eyes slowly closed. The deep ebony black falling around her shoulders was new, but hair color didn't matter to me. Whether her hair was the bright blue she'd worn when we'd first met or her natural color like now, she was the same woman.

No, I amended. She wasn't the same, but it had nothing to do with her appearance. She'd changed her hair color and removed her eyebrow and bellybutton piercings, but not because I'd asked her to. She'd done it because she was feeling more comfortable in her own skin. It was funny. Most people assumed that, because of the way she dressed, she had to be confident, not caring what others thought. I knew, however, that while some of her appearance was personal preference, some of it had been her way of shielding herself from being hurt again. A disguise.

Anger flared up inside me and I tightened my arms around her. I hated knowing that she'd spent the first thirteen years of her life being abused in ways that I didn't want to imagine. The problem was, it didn't matter whether or not I wanted to think about the past or not. Images were already seared into my brain. She'd told me only a fraction of what she'd suffered and it had been worse than anything I could've dreamed up. I wasn't a naïve person, far from it, but I never would have thought someone could do such awful things to a child. Especially the child's mother. I supposed it was more the difference between concept and reality. Knowing it on an intellectual level was one thing. Loving someone who'd actually had those things done to her was quite another.

Love.

I smiled as my fingers lazily trailed up and down her spine. I'd thought I'd been in love with Lara

Roache, so much so that I'd been ready to marry her. When I'd found her in bed with another woman, I'd been devastated, heart-broken. I knew now, though, that what I'd felt for Lara had been only a fraction of true love. Losing Lara had made me swear off relationships, determined that I wouldn't put my heart out there until I found someone I thought was worth the risk.

Then I'd fallen in love with Jenna Lang, this strong, vulnerable, amazing woman. I wasn't entirely sure how it had happened. I wasn't looking for love. In fact, I'd been close to giving up. Not just on love, but on everything. I'd had family, friends, a thriving business doing what I loved, and no-strings-attached sex with gorgeous women...and it hadn't been enough.

I kissed the top of Jenna's head. I knew she sometimes felt like I'd rescued her, helped her heal from her past, but she had no idea that she'd saved me just as much. I might not have been subjected to the horrors of her past, but I'd essentially stopped living and I hadn't even known it until I'd met her.

I'd heard all the clichés, but I'd never truly understood any of them until Jenna had come into my life. It had been like I'd been asleep all my life until I saw her. Like the sun breaking through a cloudy sky. Seeing in color instead of black and white. Like the freshest breath of air. Water for a dying man. Every cliché I'd ever heard.

My chest ached with the strength of emotion coursing through me. It hadn't just hit me fast, it had hit me hard. After Lara, I'd tried telling myself that I'd be careful the next time I met someone I might care about, but I'd had no choice in the matter. I'd fallen for Jenna so quickly that it had almost frightened me, and it had been torture holding back when all I'd wanted to do nearly from that first moment was kiss her until neither of us could breathe. I'd seen how fragile she was beneath that tough exterior and hadn't wanted to scare her off with the depth of what I felt.

Even so, I knew people thought we were moving too fast. I'd only known her for four months and I'd already asked her to move in with me. What I hadn't told anyone was that, if I'd had my way, I would've kept her with me after what happened with Christophe. I'd known before then that I'd loved her, but that had made it clear to me how much.

When I thought about how close I'd come to letting her get hurt, to losing her, I couldn't breathe. I'd never have forgiven myself if Christophe had harmed her. I didn't even want to think about something worse than an assault.

I wrapped my body more securely around her, loving that she trusted me enough to let me hold her while she slept. I was so grateful that she'd agreed to move in with me. I needed her to be there, needed to know that she was safe. And I needed her here for me. She made me a better man, a stronger man.

I didn't know what I'd do if I lost her, but it wouldn't be good. I wasn't sure I could survive it. Or if I'd want to. In a short time, she'd become my life, and I could never go back to the way I'd been.

Chapter 1

Four Months Earlier

She'd been watching me for two months, peeking up at me through lowered lashes as other men led her past me. I'd been frequenting The Den for a few weeks, choosing whichever free Subs caught my attention, when she'd appeared. She was small, barely five feet tall, and if she weighed a hundred pounds, I'd have been shocked.

While I didn't exactly have a type when it came to physical appearance – all hair colors, eye colors and skin tones welcome – I did generally prefer women who were at least average height and had some curves or muscles. Women like her, ones who were so petite, I always felt like I had to hold back or run the risk of breaking them. And while I was a Dom and enjoyed some S&M play, I wasn't into causing real pain.

Tonight, she'd apparently decided she wasn't going to take no for an answer. I'd taken a seat at my usual table and ordered a drink, then I'd seen her.

Like a good Sub, she'd had her head down and hadn't looked anyone in the eye, but instead of staying at the fringes, waiting for a Dom to approach her, she came straight towards me.

Her long, strawberry blonde hair was done up with pins, leaving just a few strands free to frame a youthful face. I knew that no one in The Den was under twenty-one, but she barely looked old enough to be out of high school. What she was wearing, however, was far from high school dress code.

The skirt was leather but barely enough material to be considered a skirt. I suspected that if she'd sat down, I'd know if she was wearing panties. Her top was a corset that ended above her belly button and pushed her small breasts up enough to give her the illusion of cleavage. Her heels were dangerously high and her legs bare. The only accessory she wore was a leather collar around her neck.

Her name was Sarah, though I suspected it probably wasn't her real name. That was fine; I hadn't told her mine at all. I'd laid all that out before we'd left The Den. No last names. No follow-up. When we were finished, I'd have a cab take her home. She wasn't to come back to the house or try to find me. If we met at the club and decided to play together again, that was fine, but we weren't a couple and we would never be one. If I ever fell in love again, it wouldn't be with someone I met at a bdsm club.

Sarah made a noise, drawing my attention back to her. The sound was muffled by the ball gag I'd strapped on a couple minutes ago. I didn't intend to keep it in very long since I enjoyed hearing the sounds and noises that came with good sex, but I'd wanted to truss Sarah up a bit first. I didn't always have partners who wanted to be bound and gagged.

She was spread-eagle on the bed, still clothed, though her skirt was rucked up enough to confirm my previous suspicions that she wasn't wearing anything underneath. I was also pretty sure she had her clit pierced, which made me wonder if her nipples were pierced too. While I wasn't sure I'd want to date someone with those body parts pierced, they did have their uses during bdsm play.

I pulled my shirt over my head and ran my fingers through my dark hair to smooth it down. I needed a haircut. It was starting to get that slightly wild look that most people didn't consider very professional. As Rylan Archer, CEO of Archer Enterprises, I did have a public face to maintain. I rolled my eyes as I thought of the magazine that had called a couple weeks ago. They didn't just want me to be rich and smart, apparently I was hot too, and that made me one of business' most eligible bachelors. I wasn't stupid. I knew I was good-looking. Eyes that were a unique shade of blue-violet, tall, in shape...I'd been fending off advances from would-be girlfriends even before I became a billionaire.

I tossed my shirt onto the floor and then removed my pants. I kept my black boxer-briefs on though. I wouldn't be getting completely naked until she was stripped and begging to be fucked.

I climbed onto the bed and began to undo the corset. I loved the front-fastening ones for situations such as this. It made it a lot easier to get to what I wanted. I took my time, undoing each lace tie from the bottom up, exposing tanned skin inch by inch. I skimmed my fingers across her stomach and felt her catch her breath, or at least as much as she could.

I looked up at her. "Are your nipples pierced?" She nodded.

"If you can stay still while I play with them, I'll take out the ball gag. Then I'll make you come." I nipped at her stomach and she jerked. "But if you can't, I'll take out the gag and replace it with my cock."

She nodded in understanding, eyes practically glowing with lust.

I let the two sides of the corset fall apart, exposing small but perky breasts. Her nipples were small as well, the color of milk chocolate. Through each one was a gold hoop, thicker than regular nipple rings, enough so that I suspected they'd been specially made.

I flicked one with a finger and Sarah didn't move. "Good girl." I poked the tip of my finger into the hoop. "Did you have these made?" She nodded. "Let me guess, strong enough to put weights on?" She nodded again, cheeks flushing.

I might not have been into the whole weighting thing, but hey, as long as it was consensual, who was I to judge what got someone off. I grasped the hoop between my thumb and forefinger and slowly twisted it. I heard the muffled moan, but she didn't move. I watched her carefully for any sign of stopping. She'd set a couple hard limits, but unless she used her safe word – apples – or snapped her fingers, she was up for pretty much anything.

I leaned down and flicked my tongue against the hoop, then circled her nipple, watching it harden into a tight little point. I covered her other breast with my hand, squeezing as I took her nipple and some of her breast into my mouth. I sucked hard on the sensitive flesh, sliding my lips closed until only her nipple remained in my mouth. She was making all sorts of noises, but she didn't move. Damn, she had some serious self-control. My tongue played with the cool metal, warming it. When I took the hoop between my teeth and tugged, every muscle in her body tensed.

I released her and looked up. Her expression was strained, but she wasn't indicating that she'd had too much, so I switched breasts, repeating with my mouth what I'd done once before. My fingers quickly found her free nipple, rolling and tugging at it before moving to the ring. I felt the tension in her body, heard the muffled whimpers. I was impressed by her control as I used teeth and tongue and fingers to twist and pull until her nipples were swollen and red.

I sat back on my knees and admired my handiwork. Sarah's hands were clenched into fists and her breath came in sharp pants. Her muscles trembled with the effort of keeping herself from moving, but she'd managed it.

"Good girl," I said as I leaned up to take the ball gag out of her mouth. Her teeth had left marks on the rubber.

"Thank you, Sir," she gasped, then worked to control her breathing. I watched her force air into her nose and out of her sexy mouth.

"Now, to give you your reward." I flicked one of her nipple rings. "You can come whenever you want, and be as loud as you want, but you're still not allowed to move."

She swallowed hard, but didn't argue. It was clear she'd been well-trained, which was just how I liked them. I didn't want a novice. I didn't have the time to put into training someone. I rarely saw the same woman more than once. The more experienced she was in the lifestyle, the better. It was all about the now.

I reached between her legs, my hand disappearing under the tiny bit of skirt that covered her. She moaned as my fingers slipped between her slick folds. She was soaked. I slid a finger inside her as I brushed my thumb over her clit. It was pierced, the metal hot from her body. Her pussy clamped down on me and my cock hardened at the thought of being inside her soon. Not yet though. I fully intended to have fun with her before I came.

I pressed my thumb harder against her clit as I worked a second finger inside her. She swore and her thigh muscles began to quiver. She was close

84

and I fully intended to make her move. I wanted to feel her mouth around my cock.

I shifted, twisting my arm so that I could curl my fingers inside her, pressing against her g-spot. Her body jerked and she keened as she came. I looked up at her, watching her face contort as she pulled against her restraints. Her skin darkened as she flushed and she bit her bottom lip, muscles clenching, then relaxing. I kept up steady pressure on both her clit and that spot inside her until her moans of pleasure turned into whimpers. Only then did I remove my hand from between her legs, but not before giving the metal bar in her clit a final flick. Her entire body shuddered and another whimper fell from her mouth.

I held my hand up to her and she opened her mouth obediently. As she sucked my fingers clean, each pull went straight to my cock. She was thorough, tasting every little bit of my skin until I pulled my fingers out.

I climbed off of the bed and went to one of the chests of drawers. I had lots of different types of toys. Whips, crops, floggers of all sizes and shapes were in the drawer I opened. I considered a flogger, imagining for a moment the way pink stripes would look on her skin, then picked up a crop instead.

Sarah's eyes darkened when she saw it, but it was the kind of change that came with lust rather than fear. I walked over to the bed and ran the tip of the crop from her belly button up to the slight dip between her breasts.

"I'm going to give you a choice." I traced her lips with the crop. "As punishment for moving, you can either have the crop or my cock."

Her eyes flicked down to where my cock was curving up towards my stomach through the material of my boxers. I wasn't huge, but I wasn't small either. A bit over average in length and width. Sarah licked her lips and I knew what she wanted.

"Before you decide, I'll expect you to take all of it." I pushed my boxers down my hips and wrapped my fist around my swollen shaft, stroking it a couple of times to make sure she got a good look at what I had to offer. "Every last inch."

"And if I can't?" Her voice was low, with just a hint of an accent. Some sort of European, I believed. She hadn't spoken much and her moans were international.

"If you can't, or you change your mind, then you get the crop, but only half of what I was going to give."

The glint in her eyes told me she would do what I wanted her to do. "I'll try, Sir. I'll try to take your dick."

"Good girl." I set the crop down on the bed and climbed up, moving so that I was straddling her chest.

I put one hand on the wall above the bed to steady myself and used the other to cradle her head and help support her neck. The head of my cock slipped between her lips and I slowly moved forward. I wanted her to change her mind so I could use the crop, but I wasn't going to shove forward and hurt her. Being a Dom meant understanding that fine line.

"That's it," I said as I made a couple shallow thrusts, enjoying the heat of her mouth and the pressure of her lips. There was no way she'd be able to take all of me. Even if she could take me into her throat, her mouth wouldn't open wide enough to get to the base. She was just too small.

I leaned forward, giving her another inch, then drew back, fucking her mouth in a slow in and out. I pushed further with each thrust, going a bit deeper each time. When I was at the back of her throat, I glanced at her hands. She didn't snap her fingers so I kept going. My cock was throbbing now, eager to be fully encased in the soft, wet heat of her mouth. She didn't gag as I slipped into her throat, but I could see her lips straining around me, her mouth open wide. When she had only an inch more to go, I heard her fingers snap. Her signal to stop.

Immediately, I slid out of her mouth. She gasped for air for a few seconds and I waited to see what she had to say. I didn't think she was completely calling off, but I wasn't going to do anything else until I knew for certain.

"Crop." Her voice was rough, but the word was clear. As clear as the desire in her eyes.

I nodded and got off the bed. I waited until she was breathing normally and her eyes had stopped watering, then picked up the crop. I had no doubt she'd known she couldn't take it, but had wanted to try just so she could get both the cock and the crop.

"Five hits," I said. "On each tit."

She shivered, her smile communicating her anticipation.

"And five on your pussy."

Her eyes widened, and her hips lifted, but she didn't protest. If anything, the desire in her eyes increased.

"Am I allowed to come, Sir?" she asked.

I considered telling her no, but I'd never really been into orgasm denial with my one-time flings. I'd done a bit of that with Lara, but it wasn't anything I wanted to get into with someone I didn't know well enough to read their body. It was a fine art, knowing when a woman was going to come and being able to stop at the right time.

"Whenever you want," I said. "And as many times as you can." I held up the crop. "But after I'm done, I'm going to fuck you until I come."

"Thank you, Sir." She curled her fingers into fists and I knew she was preparing herself for what was to come.

I didn't use a crop very often, and rarely on the more sensitive parts of the anatomy, but there were some who enjoyed it, and Sarah's smile said she was definitely one of them. I flicked my wrist and heard the crack against her breast, followed immediately by the soft pained sound she made. A small red patch appeared on her skin.

I alternated between her breasts for the first six blows, then landed the first one on her nipple. She cried out, body twisting instinctively. The first one on the other nipple received a similar response. I made the last one on each harder than the others and she wailed. I was suddenly very glad I hadn't taken her to a hotel. I doubted neighboring rooms would've appreciated this as fully as I did.

Sarah took great gulping breaths, each one making her breasts jiggle. Her eyes were wide as she watched me pull her skirt up around her waist, completely exposing her bare pussy. Her skin glistened and I could see the tip of her clit peeking out, just a hint of the silver bar with it. Perfect. I hadn't wanted to spread her folds and hit her clit directly, but there was enough of it visible for me to know it'd get some punishment.

I kept the first two blows low enough that her pink lips caught all of it. Still a shock, I was sure, but not as much as what was coming. The third was higher, but not as hard, giving her a few seconds to prepare herself for what was happening next. The fourth hit her directly and her entire body jerked hard enough that I was glad I'd chosen soft restraints rather than handcuffs. Her body tensed and her face contorted into the beautiful mask of orgasm. She screamed and her body twisted again. I made the last one count, landing perfectly, even as she continued to ride out her climax.

While her overwhelmed body twitched and shook, half-sobs coming out with every shuddering breath, I got a condom from the bedside table and rolled it on. By the time I was on the bed again, kneeling between her spread legs, I was nearly painfully hard and she was coherent enough to consent.

I'd stretched her well with my fingers before and knew she could take all of me without any damage, so I gripped her hips and buried myself with one thrust. My pelvic bone hit against her swollen clit and she swore. My strokes were deep and hard, my fingers digging into her small hips, and she begged for it to be harder and faster. She came again after only a couple minutes, and I kept going, drawing out her orgasm until the pressure inside me was too much and I exploded. My eyes closed and I let the pleasure give me what I sought. A few precious moments of peace.

Chapter 2

Autumn in Fort Collins was my favorite time of year. The mountains were covered with trees, some that would stay the deep green of pine while others would burst into reds and oranges and yellows. The weather had started to cool at the end of August and now, halfway through September, the temperature was perfect.

The last couple years, however, I'd found less and less time to appreciate the beauty of the city and the season. Now, as I drove from my house in to the office, I barely noticed anything around me. I had too much on my mind. That had been what fucking Sarah had been for, to clear my head so that I could figure out what to do about the newest problem my company was having. Unfortunately, enjoyable as it had been, sex with Sarah hadn't done much in the way of getting me out of my head for more than a few seconds. Things had still been there, nagging at the back of my mind.

It was times like these that I really missed Curt. He'd been with me since the beginning, the public face of Archer Enterprises. He'd taken care of meet and greets with clients, public relations, interviews, leaving me to do what I did best: not deal with people. I'd been happy sitting in my office, working on code and systems. Then, about a year and a half ago, he'd had an accident, spent some time in a coma, and then moved to the Bahamas with his wife. I didn't begrudge him the early retirement, especially after everything he'd been through. It didn't make me miss him any less.

"Rylan!"

I turned as I heard my name and put on a fake smile. "Emmaline." The twenty-three year-old was bubbly, high energy, both things that were positive, but not something I was fond of first thing in the morning. I'd never been much of a morning person.

"I have your coffee ready." She beamed at me, her turquoise eyes shining.

I accepted the cup. "Thank you." A bit of an awkward silence followed. "Well, work to do."

I headed towards the elevator, hoping she wouldn't follow. She wasn't my assistant, but she still brought me coffee almost every morning. I'd gotten the impression she wanted something romantic from me, but I wasn't about to go there. Even if Emmaline was the kind of person I'd want to date, the fact that I was her boss would've immediately negated it. As it was, she wasn't the sort of woman I would want to be with. She'd never done anything specific, but I'd always had the feeling she wasn't quite as genuine and nice as she tried to make me think.

"Rylan!"

I sighed. It was a man's voice this time and one that I recognized. Dark hair and eyes, slouched shoulders. Christophe Constantine was a good employee. Hard-working, on time, never complained. I just wasn't in the mood for conversation.

"Package for you." He held out a small square box.

"Thanks, Christophe."

He smiled, gave me a nod and hurried off. He was my assistant, but he also did odd errands for other people at the company. I was all about work efficiency and keeping busy. I didn't care quite so much about job titles.

I breathed a sigh of relief when I walked out of the elevator and into my office. I had an open door policy with my employees, but no one abused it. Unless something came up, I had at least a couple hours to myself. I put the package down on the desk and walked around to my chair. I knew what was in it. New business cards that only had my name on them instead of Curt's as well. I hadn't wanted to order them, but I'd known that I had to do it. Somehow, seeing just my name felt more final than it had when I'd accepted his resignation.

If I hadn't already needed to talk to him, this would've made me want to call him. Curt wasn't my best friend, but he had been the closest person to me here. I sat down and picked up my phone. He answered on the third ring.

"Rylan, how're things in the States?"

I smiled despite myself. Curt had always had that effect on me. He'd been the guy who'd kept me from taking myself too seriously. That's why he'd been such a great public face. He was personable, likable, at ease with the press and with anyone else he happened to talk to.

"They're fine, Curt. How're you doing?"

"Shirley and I are great. Having drinks on the beach every night."

I laughed. "You sound bored out of your mind."

He laughed along with me. "I have to admit, there are times when I do miss a good old nine to five."

"Well, your nine to five misses you too."

"Ah." His voice had a knowing note to it. "What is it?"

"I've been informed that Archer Enterprises has an image problem." I jumped right in. Another thing that had made Curt and I such great partners. Our transition from small talk to business had always been quick.

"Really? Who told you that?" Judging by the lack of surprise in his voice, this wasn't news to him. Curt always kept up on things.

"Only half the blogs and papers on the West Coast," I said wryly. "An issue with one of our games."

"*Bridger's Doom*," Curt said. "An obscene easter egg on the fourth level."

"I fired the programmer who did it," I said. "And I recalled the product, offered a full refund as well as a replacement once the glitch is fixed."

"But you didn't have a press conference. You didn't apologize," Curt said. "You should've been making the rounds. Interviews, talk shows, the whole nine yards."

I sighed and ran my hand through my hair. "You know I'm no good at this, Curt. I'm not the guy who charms crowds. I'm fine one-on-one, with people who speak my language, but I suck when some reporter asks me a bunch of shit that has nothing to do with work."

"It's been eighteen months, Rylan," he said. "Maybe it's time for you to hire someone for public relations."

"And what are they going to do?" I asked. "Tell me the right things to say; which programs to go on. They won't let me work in peace."

He was silent for a moment, his voice soft when he spoke again, "When was the last time you went out? Spent time with friends?"

"I saw Zeke a couple weeks ago," I said, my voice lifted in defense. "And I had a date last night."

"A date?" Curt sounded amused. "Rylan, I know you. That wasn't a date."

"What does it matter?" I asked, annoyed for a reason I couldn't quite explain. "My social life is my own business."

"You take things far too seriously," Curt said. "What happened to the guy who used to hack into the school's mainframe and play with the Christmas lights?"

"He started his own company," I said as if my answer explained everything. My annoyance faded as quickly as it had come. I had been that guy once. Now, responsibility took over. Even when I was with my friends, I was thinking about work. I doubted any of them noticed, but Curt knew the truth. Work was all I had.

"Rylan, you need to take it easy. What's the point of all this if you can't enjoy it with someone?"

"I enjoy it just fine," I said. "You should've seen the woman I was with last night."

Even as I said it, I felt the lie. I didn't let myself acknowledge it though. Fucking someone wasn't the same as sharing my life, but it was what I had. I'd opened my heart to someone once. Unless I was certain she was worth it, I wouldn't do it again.

Chapter 3

"I'm glad you called. I was beginning to think you'd thrown me over for code."

Zeke Wesson had been my best friend since childhood and I knew him almost as well as I knew myself. Light brown hair, moss green eyes. We were about the same size, but he'd always been bulkier than me. People usually described him more as the ruggedly handsome type. Whatever he was, the two of us never had any issues picking up women.

Which was what we were doing now.

If an intense bdsm session with Sarah hadn't been enough to make me relax, maybe what I actually needed was something a bit tamer. Something that took me back to a time when things were simpler. Just me and Zeke at a bar, having a drink, trying to pick up a couple of women.

"It's been a busy year," I said. "What with Curt quitting and everything."

"I'm just glad the holidays are coming up," he said. "I'm thinking, big Christmas Eve party this year at your place and then an even bigger New

Year's Eve party. Maybe see if CSU will let us rent out Moby Arena. I'm talking a live band, hundreds of people." He grinned and lifted his eyebrows. "CSU co-eds?"

I shook my head and took a swig of my beer. "You do realize that you're going to be thirty next June, right?"

Zeke flipped me off and grinned. "Just means I need to pack in twice as much fun before I become an old man."

I scanned the bar. "And you're not even considering settling down any time soon?"

He laughed. "You're kidding, right?" His expression changed slightly and, for a moment, I couldn't figure out what he was thinking. Then his smile was back. "Come on, Rylan, why would I want to give up all this? I mean, I've never met a woman I could stand for more than a couple weeks. You think I could find one I'd want to be with forever?" He leaned across the table and clinked his beer bottle against mine. "You're pretty much the only person I could imagine being around that long."

I shrugged. I had to admit, in a way, he was right. When I thought about plans for the future, if I ever had anyone with me, it was either Zeke or Suzette, my younger sister. Since Lara and I had broken up, I hadn't let myself imagine a future with anyone else.

"What about them?" Zeke gestured with his bottle.

I followed the direction. At the end of the bar

were two women, one with auburn hair, the other light brown. Both were watching us with open admiration. They were both cute. Not in a drop-dead gorgeous kind of way, but enough to get attention from the other men in the bar.

I shrugged. "Why not?" I was looking for sex, not companionship. Personality really didn't matter much and the pair were attractive enough. Plus, Zeke tended to be picky when it came to women, so if he liked them, I wasn't going to argue.

"Flip to see who goes in first?" Zeke grinned as he pulled a quarter from his pocket.

"Heads," I called as he flipped it in the air.

He caught it, looked down and grinned. "Tails. Guess you're up."

"You have a preference for the red-head or the brunette?" I asked as I stood.

He looked at them again. "The brunette."

The brunette, it turned out, was Robin. The red-head was Janette. They'd come from Kansas State to visit their boyfriends at CSU only to find said boyfriends in bed...with each other. I could definitely sympathize, though I didn't plan on sharing my similar story. Zeke, however, had absolutely no compunctions about entertaining the ladies with my unfortunate dating history.

"You poor thing." Janette put her hand over mind and leaned against me. She was about average in build, and if the breasts pressing against my arm were any indication, she was wearing a padded bra in an attempt to make that part of her anatomy more than average. I never minded the size of a woman's breasts, but wearing something padded always felt a bit like I was being lied to.

"And he hasn't had a serious girlfriend since," Zeke finished up. He gave me a half-drunken grin.

"Zeke forgot to mention that he's never had a serious girlfriend." I glared at him. I was a bit buzzed, but he was working his way towards serious intoxication.

"So you're both the love 'em and leave 'em type?" Robin asked, inching closer to Zeke.

"You could say that," I said dryly. "We like to have fun without any strings attached."

"You know," Janette said. "Robin and I were just saying that we needed to find two hot guys and have a seriously sexy fling with them. To get our minds off our boyfriends. Ex-boyfriends."

"Well, you don't want to do anything you'd regret," Zeke said. His words weren't slurred, but they were blunted. "You sure you guys won't get back together?"

I raised an eyebrow at him. Was he seriously trying to talk these two out of sex?

"Considering what they were doing when we walked in the room," Robin said. "I very much doubt it."

"They could've just been experimenting," Zeke pointed out. "Or they were drunk and horny. It happens."

Robin gave him a look and then glanced at me. "Has it ever happened with the two of you?"

"No," I said. "I have no problem with people loving who they love, but I'm straight."

"Me too," Zeke added quickly. "Just wanted you to be sure that's what you want."

"I know what I want." Janette put her hand on my thigh and squeezed.

"Me too," Robin practically purred.

Judging by the way Zeke jumped, Robin had grabbed something of his too. I was certain it hadn't been his leg.

"We're sharing a hotel room," Janette said. "Unless it bothers you guys to be in the same room."

I looked at Zeke and he shrugged before draining the last of his beer. "We're game if you are."

Less than fifteen minutes later, we were in a semi-dark room, Janette and me on one bed, Zeke and Robin on the other. My shirt was somewhere on the floor and I was working on getting Janette's over her head. Her mouth, however, had other ideas. Her tongue was in my mouth, as demanding as her hands were on my body. Finally, I grabbed her wrists and pinned them above her head. She gasped in surprise, then moaned as I nipped at her bottom lip.

"Don't move," I said quietly. I couldn't see much of her face, but her head nodded and she didn't move her hands when I released them.

I quickly pulled off her shirt, then moved to her jeans. Out of the corner of my eye, I caught a glimpse of Zeke stripping an eager Robin. Her hands were all over him and I could feel the tension radiating off of him in waves. I turned my attention back to Janette, pulled down her panties and tossed them aside. Her creamy skin gleamed white in the dim light.

"Take off your bra," I said as I pulled off my own pants and underwear. Before dropping them, I pulled a condom out of my pocket and set it on the bed. I considered tossing one over to Zeke, but I decided against it. If he needed one, he'd ask. Besides, the chances of him not having one were slim. From the way he talked, he had sex almost every night.

Janette already had her legs spread when I turned back to her and I settled between them, stretching out with my legs half-hanging over the edge of the bed. I looked up at her as I put her knees over my shoulders. She had her hands on her breasts, rubbing them, playing with her nipples. I couldn't see much of her face, but I could feel her eyes on me.

A masculine groan from the next bed told me that Zeke was on the receiving end of something quite pleasurable. I lowered my head and pressed my mouth against Janette's pussy. She whimpered and made an inarticulate sound that mingled with what Zeke was making when I slid my tongue between her folds. I wanted her to be louder than Zeke. Might've been a bit of chauvinistic arrogance, but I wasn't going to apologize for it.

I found her clit easily enough and began circling it with my tongue. Her body writhed on the bed above me. I was pretty sure I heard her say someone else's name, but I ignored it. I didn't care if she called me by her boyfriend's name. I didn't plan on seeing her again after tonight. Hell, I didn't even care if her name wasn't Janette. As long as she was overage and consenting. Nothing else mattered.

I shifted my body so that I could slide a finger inside her. She was already wet and I could feel her body quivering around me. A second finger joined the first and she tensed. I took her clit between my lips, teasing it as I waited for her to relax. When she did, I began to slowly pump my fingers in and out, stretching her in preparation for what was to come.

"On your hands and knees."

I heard Zeke's strained voice above Janette's moans. Then, a few seconds later, a gasp came from the next bed. I didn't need much of an imagination to know that he'd just entered her.

I crooked my fingers, searching for that spot inside her that would make her come. Her hips bucked up as I found it and I rubbed my fingertips against it until she cried out and I felt her climax, her body clenching, her thighs tightening around my head. I worked her through it with fingers and mouth until she was still and gasping for breath. Then I moved back.

As I opened the condom wrapper and rolled it on, I glanced over at the other bed. Robin and Zeke seemed to be enjoying themselves, if the noise was any indication. I could only make out the shadows of them. Robin on all fours, Zeke behind her, pounding into her with surprising force. She didn't appear to mind though, pushing her ass back towards him to meet every thrust.

I looked down at Janette and caught a glimpse of a smile, before she looked over to watch the other couple as well. I grasped her hips and lifted her so that her ass was resting on my thighs. She wrapped her legs around my waist as I positioned her. She made a small sound in the back of her throat as I pushed just the tip of my cock inside her. Slowly, I pulled her towards me, letting her adjust to my size. By the time I reached the end of her, she was shaking, her breath coming in gasps.

"Say when." My fingers dug into her hips with the strain of waiting. She was tight around me, the wet heat almost too much.

Fortunately, I didn't have to wait long.

"I'm okay," she said. Her voice was breathless, but I didn't detect any pain.

I moved slowly for the first couple strokes, not picking up the pace until she began to raise her hips to meet me. Only then did I hold her still and began to thrust into her hard and fast. I rolled my hips every few strokes, rubbing her clit against the base of my cock until she cried out.

From the other bed, I heard Robin make a sound that was halfway between a yell and a squeal. A grunting sound from Zeke followed, telling me that they'd both finished. I shifted my weight, leaning forward slightly so that every thrust would hit Janette deep and my pelvic bone would put pressure on her clit.

Her back arched, a nearly soundless cry falling from her lips as she came again. I didn't let up, slamming into her even harder than before. I was close. I felt the heat inside me, coiling into a tight knot of anticipation. Her pussy fluttered around me, muscles spasming from the overstimulation. I squeezed my eyes shut, unsure of who I was trying to see, only that I knew it wasn't Janette.

Finally, I came, tensing as the pleasure coursed through me, heat and electricity combining to give me momentary relief. But that's all it was, momentary. As soon as I started to come down, the world was back and I was awkwardly aware of Zeke and Robin watching.

As I flopped back on the bed to catch my breath, I wondered if this had been such a good idea after all.

Chapter 4

Part of me wished Curt would've been at work on Monday just so I could tell him that his suggestion of going out and having a life was completely fucked up. It hadn't really done much of anything except make me even more exhausted than I normally felt after working most of the weekend. I hadn't gotten much sleep, and what I had gotten hadn't been very restful. I hadn't gone to the gym either and that didn't help matters much. I was far from obsessive when it came to working out, but I liked to stay in shape, and the exercise always helped me clear my head and get ready for the new week.

Instead of that, however, my brain was still foggy and I had a slight headache. Even as I walked into the office, I felt irritable for no good reason. This was going to be one of those days, I just knew it. The kind of day that the slightest little thing was going to annoy the hell out of me and I would end up snapping at someone, regretting it later.

"Here's your coffee." Emmaline smiled brightly as she held out my cup.

"Thank you." It took way too much effort not to sound annoyed even though she hadn't really done anything. Bringing me coffee was going above and beyond. "Have you seen Christophe?"

"He was taking something up to your office last I saw him." She followed me to the elevators. "I didn't think you'd mind."

"I don't," I said. And I really didn't. If I couldn't trust Christophe in my office, I couldn't trust anyone. "How's the beta testing going?"

Emmaline was part of a group of employees who were monitoring beta testing of a couple of new games as well as a minimum security firewall. They weren't programmers, but rather collected the data, collated it, and wrote up a report about the various products. Technically, she was more of the assistant to the group, running errands, that kind of thing, but she also paid attention to what was going on and offered her opinion when she could.

"It's going well," she said.

She seemed pleased that I'd asked her rather than one of the senior members of the team.

"*Guardian's Cross* has been testing well in its demographic," she continued. "And it doesn't seem to have too many glitches. I think someone mentioned some sort of problem with a graphic, but nothing big. *Legions* has been having problems on level five, but Nadine said she'd be able to get it fixed before the launch."

I nodded, taking mental notes as she kept going, telling me other stats and tidbits she'd gleaned from the group as well as her own insights. One of the reasons I'd asked her, aside from the fact that she'd been right here, had been because I knew she'd give me everything. The others in the group might've tried to gloss over some things, figuring if they could get them fixed, I didn't need to know. I wanted to know though. If programmers were turning out faulty products, it was my job to deal with it. Glitches happened to the best of us, but repetitive issues meant I needed to take a closer look at people.

The elevator dinged and the doors slid open.

"Thank you, Emmaline," I said sincerely. "I really appreciate you being so thorough."

I had a mental list of things to check, but put them aside when I reached my office. Christophe was at my desk, a serious expression on his face. He looked up when I came in, cheeks flushing slightly.

"Sorry, Rylan. I knew you'd want to see this as soon as you came in and I didn't want to risk not catching you until later because I was off on another errand."

"It's not a big deal." I glanced down at the manila envelope on my desk. I wasn't close enough yet to see the address. "Who's it from?"

"The Justice Department," Christophe said nervously. "Is something wrong?"

I shook my head, relieved. If it was coming to me rather than our lawyer, it didn't have anything to do with the easter egg issue. If it had been a summons or something like that, it would've gone straight to me. The fact that Christophe had it meant it couldn't be too bad.

I took a gulp of my coffee and sat down. "Thanks, Christophe."

"Anything I can get for you?" he asked.

"If you could start a pot of coffee, I'd appreciate it," I said, not looking up at him. "Caffeinated." I'd never get through today with decaf.

I opened the envelope as Christophe went to do as I'd asked. It wasn't anything bad. In fact, it was very good. I'd been selected as one of the frontrunners to receive a contract from the Department of Justice for digital security. I'd forgotten that I'd even put a bid in for it. I'd done it the week before Curt's accident, so I'd been a bit preoccupied at the time. No surprise it had taken the Justice Department so long to get back to me.

I smiled as I leaned back in my chair and called up my latest security program. I was still tired, but at least the day was looking up. The system I was working on now might be exactly what the Justice Department needed. There were still bugs in the system, but the big glitches had already been worked out. I hoped I could try it out on my system here within the week.

Like most things at Archer Enterprises, the program wasn't the work of a single person, though I'd done most of the detail work. I had programmers who wrote the base code for pretty much every system we put out. Then there were the second level people who specialized in certain areas like games or security. In groups of two or three, they wrote the rest of the code, and then sent the program to be reviewed by a select set of people.

I'd had other CEOs tell me I was crazy to let that many people have their hands on each program, but I'd found it worked much better. Not only was each person only working in their area of expertise, but they held each other accountable. The field we were in was a competitive one and if anyone saw someone else slip up, they'd point it out in a nanosecond. The multi-layered approach also allowed for teamwork within the competition. I always gave bonuses for work well done, which meant they had to work together if they wanted those bonuses.

I frowned as I looked at the time logs for work done on the security program. One particular programmer seemed to be logging extra hours, but doing it alone rather than with his assigned team. It wasn't strange that someone seemed to be trying to show off by working overtime – that was fairly common. What was strange was that it was Ned Baker.

Ned was one of the quietest, most unassuming men I'd ever met. He was also a lot older than most of the other programmers. Well into his fifties, Ned had been on the cutting edge of technology from moment one. He'd not only been coding on some of the first personal computers, but had kept up with changing technology.

That left another option. One I really didn't want

to consider. Someone else was using Ned's information to work on a system they hadn't been authorized for. If that was the case, it meant two things. Not only did I have someone in the company who was up to no good, but my security technicians hadn't caught on yet.

I had three, two part-timers and one who worked full time. He was supposed to be in charge of the digital security here, making sure all the electronic records were accurate. If someone was using Ned's log-in, Truman should've caught it.

I frowned. Truman might not know Ned very well, so I did have to consider the possibility that it was an honest mistake. Still, something in my gut told me that I had a problem at Archer Enterprises and I needed to figure out what it was before something bad happened. When you worked at a place like this, bad didn't necessarily mean someone slipping an obscene image into a game. It could be federal indictment kind of bad. The last thing I needed after the recent flood of bad press was the NSA or FBI breathing down my neck.

I was tempted to simply fire Truman and hire someone else who could do things the right way. I didn't like the guy very much, but he had been the most qualified candidate who'd applied for the job. Plus, I couldn't just fire him. Well, I guess I could. Technically, I would have cause if I discovered Ned hadn't made those log-ins. That part wouldn't be difficult to prove. If that was the case, it meant Truman had missed it and I could fire him on the spot. But I had a bigger reason why Truman had to stay.

I didn't have anyone else. I supposed I could've done it, but I had enough on my plate as it was. If I added security to my duties, I might as well just move into my office. I might've been a workaholic and there had been times I'd crashed here, but that would've been taking it too far.

No, I needed to first figure out what was going on with this system and who'd been logging in without permission, then I could worry about finding someone to replace Truman.

I ran my fingers through my hair and scowled. Some days, I wondered why I'd ever bothered to start a company in the first place. Sitting in a small room, music blaring while I worked on a laptop, losing myself in the numbers and beauty of code...I missed that.

Chapter 5

I hadn't even bothered with the pretense of buying a drink and taking a seat. The Den was the only club of its kind in the city and I hadn't wanted to drive the extra distance to one of the others located between here and Denver. There weren't many, and if a person wasn't in the lifestyle, they'd never know about any of them. Discretion was how people like me managed to stay respectable for the public. Stupid, in my opinion, since everything we did was between consenting adults, but people tended to get weird about things they didn't understand.

I'd been worried that I'd run into Sarah at The Den, but I'd only seen her from a distance and she'd been thoroughly involved in giving a blowjob to a hefty man in leather. The club hadn't been very full since it was a week night, but I still had variety to choose from. After only a few minutes, I spotted a Sub standing on the outside fringes of the dance floor.

A little taller than average, she wore a tiny little dress that her nice curves accentuated. Long, straight blonde hair, the kind of platinum blonde that usually came from a box. Pouty lips and high cheekbones gave her a striking look.

It hadn't been her appearance that had made me go to her though. No, it had been the complete subservience that had gotten my attention. Her head had been down, eyes lowered so I hadn't been able to see their color. Her hands were clasped behind her back, her posture saying that she was willing to serve.

I'd approached her as I'd seen a couple other men do. They'd been turned away. I hadn't been. Lita, as she'd introduced herself, had been told by her master to stand here until a worthy man had approached. I'd considered walking away at that point, but then her master had come up and told me what he'd been looking for. Someone to dominate Lita, but not expect to ever see her again. There'd be no exchange of names, no plans made. It would be one night, and that would be all. It was nice to know I wouldn't have to worry about her wanting to see me again.

Since the last two encounters hadn't managed to completely clear my head, I'd agreed, thinking that something new might be just what I was looking for. The Dom had then given me the safe words as well as what I wasn't allowed to do to Lita. Nothing on the list had been anything I'd been into, so it was easy to agree.

I hadn't taken Lita to the house, just in case she and her Dom were thieves or worse. I didn't want to show them where I lived. I had excellent security, but being cautious was always a good idea. The hotel we were currently in was known for its discretion...plus I'd rented the penthouse, which meant it'd be less likely that any neighbors would hear me.

Well, that might've been an issue if Lita hadn't been under strict instructions from her Dom not to say a word unless it was her safe word. I had a feeling this was a game they played often, and how well she did would determine if she received a punishment or a reward.

I had no problem with that and, at the moment, Lita didn't have to worry about it since her mouth was full. The moment we'd entered the room, she'd gone down on her knees, clasped her hands behind her back, head down. As soon as I'd asked, the dress had come off, revealing she wasn't wearing anything underneath. I'd kept my clothes on, undoing my pants and pushing them down far enough to pull out my cock.

"Open."

She did as she was told and I slid my cock into her mouth. I put my hand on her head, and she stilled, waiting for me to take control. I twisted my fingers in her silky hair and pulled her towards me. I was still soft enough that she could take all of me without a problem. I held her against me as she worked her tongue around my cock as it swelled. I

117

waited for her to struggle, but she didn't. I pulled her back, letting her have a moment to breathe before I pushed forward again. Again, she took it all.

I moaned as the head of my cock slid down her throat. She swallowed, throat muscles massaging me. I put my other hand on her head, holding her still as I thrust into her mouth. I kept my strokes steady and even, not wanting to push her too far, but it still felt amazing. Her eyes stayed down, hands clasped, her body motionless.

After a few minutes, I pulled back, my cock glistening. I was hard, but didn't want sex yet. I needed to let off some steam.

"Stand up."

She did as she was told, assuming the position with her feet shoulder distance apart. I circled around her, wishing I had some of the things from my playroom. A flogger, maybe a dildo or some other toy. I wanted to see if I could make her break her silence.

I pulled my belt from my pants. I didn't use one very often, but I knew how to do it without damaging her. I ran my hand over her ass and gently squeezed. Nothing.

"I'm going to use this." I held up the belt so she could see it. "Spank your ass until it's red. Then I'm going to bend you over the bed and fuck you."

I tapped her ass with the leather of the belt, but she didn't flinch. This wasn't her first time. I took a step back and snapped the belt against one cheek. A faint pink stained her skin. I swung again, harder this time. Still, no sound. As I continued, her skin turned from pink to red, but I didn't get a gasp or a moan. Nothing to indicate if she was enjoying herself or if she bore this because she had to.

I scowled, tossing the belt onto the bed. This wasn't doing anything for me. I wanted a response, to know what she was feeling. I understood her instructions from her Master, but she didn't even appear to be struggling against the command. That was the problem with dealing with a Sub who'd been trained by a singular Dom. They knew what their Master liked, not necessarily how to please others.

I wrapped my hand around my cock and stroked it, the feel of familiar flesh under my palm. "Bend over the bed."

She walked over to the bed and did as I asked. No complaint, no attitude at all. I preferred a woman with some fire, even in a Sub. I walked up behind her and put one hand on her hip. I reached between her legs and found her wet. I guess that answered whether or not she was enjoying herself. That was something, at least, I supposed.

I rolled a condom over my cock and positioned myself at her entrance. I thought about going slow, but decided against it. I snapped my hips forward and finally felt a response. Her body jerked and she sucked in a breath. I wasn't sure it counted as a sound, but it was something.

I slammed into her, gripping her hips hard enough to bruise. Her breasts swayed with every thrust and her ass burned against my skin. I slid a hand beneath her. Her master hadn't said she couldn't come, only that she couldn't make a sound. I intended to find out if she could come silently.

My fingers found her clit easily enough, swollen and throbbing. She hissed as I brushed my finger across the sensitive flesh. I rubbed it harder, not quite rough, but hard enough that whatever she was experiencing was doubled in intensity. Fast enough to hurt. Judging by the way her body started to push back against me, that was what she liked.

I drove deep into her as I pinched her clit and she came with a moan. It wasn't a loud sound, but it was a sound nonetheless.

"Your master isn't going to be happy with you." I fisted her hair, twisting her head back to look at me.

"Since I'm to be punished already." Her voice was thick with desire. "May I ask a request?"

"Ask."

She writhed back against me. "Fuck my ass."

Not what I was expecting.

"Please," she asked.

"Don't you want to come again?"

"If you fuck my ass, I will."

I pulled out of her and took my hand from between her legs. My fingers were slick with her arousal. I pressed my finger against her asshole, working it in much easier than I'd expected.

Lita moaned. "More."

I slapped her ass with my hand, hard enough to make my palm hurt.

"Sir, please. Sir. More."

Better. I rewarded her with a second finger. She threw back her head and moaned deep in her throat.

"Sir, I'm ready, Sir." She pushed back against my hand, shoving my fingers deeper. Harder. Faster.

I knew I hadn't stretched her enough, but I withdrew my fingers and placed my cock against her. I moved slowly, finding less resistance than I normally would. She made a practice of this, I was sure. She clearly loved the pleasure pain it gave her.

"Does your master fuck you like this?" I asked as my balls rested against her hot cheeks. Her muscles gripped me, squeezed me, sucked me in.

"Only when I've been good, Sir."

"So you figured I'd give you your reward since your master's going to punish you?" I pulled back and eased forward again. Lita didn't say anything, but it didn't matter. I knew the answer anyway.

Suddenly, I just wanted this to be done. I didn't want to be here, not really. My cock was throbbing painfully, begging me to finish, so I moved faster. There was no real desire, nothing but the basic primal need for release. Lita was making all sorts of sounds of pleasure now, leaning on one arm as her fingers were busy beneath her. I could feel her body starting to tense and knew she was close again.

"Just come, already, dammit!" I growled from between gritted teeth.

As if she'd been waiting for permission or a command, she came. Her body stiffened, muscles tightening around me until I exploded. The pleasure was there, racing across my nerves, but it was a mere release of pressure, the same I'd feel if I'd had a headache go away or relieved an overly full bladder. There was no connection, nothing to make me lose myself. Nothing that made me want to do it again.

I pulled out of her ass and climbed off the bed, heading to the bathroom without a word. I climbed into the shower without waiting for it to heat up. The cold drops were like ice against my skin at first and I began to shiver. I closed my eyes as I leaned against the back wall, the tile cool against my palms. What was I doing?

Lara had broken my heart and I'd vowed to never risk that hurt again unless I found someone who was worth it. But was I really looking? Not that I thought I should be out there searching for a woman, but the places I went to find women, the women I took to bed, these weren't the kind of woman I'd ever fall for. They were distractions, one night stands. I made sure it was never anything else.

I'd always told myself that I was protecting myself, but had that been an excuse? A lie I'd told myself so I wouldn't have to face the truth? The truth was... I was absolutely petrified, but not of being hurt again. Not really. The fear was there, but it wasn't forefront in my mind. No, I was afraid that I would never fall in love for real. That I'd never find the kind of woman who I could see myself spending the rest of my life with. The kind of woman who would challenge me emotionally and intellectually. Someone I could talk to and enjoy being with. Whose body would respond to mine. The sort of woman I would be willing to give up everything for, but who would never ask it of me.

I knew she didn't exist.

I rubbed my hands over my face and reached back for the hotel shampoo. I'd thought I hadn't really known what I'd wanted, which was why I'd been on a mission to keep looking. That wasn't the case. I knew what I wanted, I just didn't think I'd ever find it.

One thing was for sure, though, what I was doing had to stop. I couldn't keep living like this. I didn't know what that would mean for the future, but I had a feeling it would mean throwing myself into work until nothing else registered.

I'd call Zeke, I decided. Talk it over with him. He'd help me figure out where I wanted to go next.

Chapter 6

"Shit!" I slammed my hand down on the desk. "Rylan?"

I looked up as Emmaline walked into my office. I encouraged my employees to see me whenever they needed something and since the elevator door led right into my office, I rarely got a warning before someone came in. It definitely kept me honest, but sometimes it could be a real pain in the ass.

"What can I do for you, Emmaline?" I gave her a genuine, albeit tired, smile.

"I had an idea for a program," she said. "And I was wondering, since the beta testing finishes up tomorrow, if I could work on my idea."

I held out a hand and she gave me the papers she'd been carrying. Everyone at Archer Enterprises had it written into their contracts that they were allowed to come up with their own programs, as long as they followed procedure. They needed to provide a clear proposal of what they wanted to accomplish and it couldn't take precedence over any contracted jobs the company received. Once the basic coding was finished, they'd submit it to me and I'd either make an offer for them to sell their program to Archer Enterprises and continue working on it with the team, or I'd tell them I wasn't interested and they'd have to cease all work on company time. I always offered more than fair compensation if I bought out the program and I'd never had anyone whose work I accepted complain. The ones I turned down, well, that was a different story, but nothing I really worried about.

I glanced over her proposal, surprised that she'd actually come up with something this sophisticated. It wasn't that I thought Emmaline wasn't intelligent, but there was a reason I had her in beta testing rather than development. Still, her proposal was decent and there was definite potential there.

"Go ahead and run with it once you're finished with your beta testing reports." I put the proposal into a folder and wrote her name on it. When she didn't make a move to leave, I looked up. "Is there anything else?"

"Oh, no, sorry." She smiled at me. "Thank you."

I gave her a nod and waited until she left before turning my attention back to the screen. I'd done a lot of the work on this particular program, writing and re-writing code until I knew it like the back of my hand. The people who'd had their hands on it last should've only been doing a basic touch-up, but there was an entirely new section I hadn't seen before.

I checked the log-in sheets against the time the code had been written and it was Ned's name that popped up again. My gut said it wasn't him, but I had to be sure and the best way to do that was to just ask. Ned was the kind of guy who couldn't lie. His ears would turn red and he wasn't able to maintain eye contact.

I picked up the phone and dialed the extension. He answered almost immediately. "Ned, it's Rylan. Could you come to my office?"

While I waited, I studied the code more carefully. I knew Ned's work. I'd been seeing it almost from day one. Every programmer had their own unique style, though to a lay-person, there'd seem to be no difference. Whoever had done this hadn't been subtle. Aside from being one of my best programmers, Ned was smart. If he'd really written this code, he would've made it much harder for me to find.

"Rylan," Ned said as he stepped off of the elevator. "Is something wrong?"

"Have a seat." I gestured to one of the chairs on the other side of my desk. "I have a couple questions I need you to answer, but I can't tell you why."

Ned looked confused, but not guilty, which I took to be a positive sign. "All right."

"Where were you last Tuesday night?" I went with the first time I'd seen his name more than average.

I watched Ned access his mental calendar, then look back at me with certainty on his face. "I was here for a while. I stayed late that night." His forehead wrinkled in concentration. "I was having a problem with my log-ins. Truman and I stayed until about six-thirty. Then I went to a talent show at my niece's high school."

"Did Truman leave with you?"

"No." He shook his head. "I was in a hurry. The show started at seven and I didn't want to be late. He said he'd finish up for me."

"And Thursday night?"

His eyes stared at the wall in thought, then zoned in and returned to mine. "Home," he said. "I left work on time, went straight home and stayed there."

I knew he was divorced and didn't have any kids, so I doubted anyone had seen him. Knowing Ned, he'd probably spent the night reading.

"Is everything all right?" His concern was evident in his voice, but it seemed totally focused on me and not on himself. Either Ned had vastly improved his acting skills or he had nothing to do with my little programming problem. I was inclined to believe the latter.

"Nothing you need to worry about," I said with a smile. "Go ahead back to your work."

He nodded. I could tell he was still confused about what was going on, but he didn't press matters. Yet another reason why I genuinely liked Ned. I waited until he left and turned back to the program on my screen.

I was glad I'd decided to check things completely

this time. On a lot of programs over the last year, I'd trusted my employees and just given things a once over. That was how the stupid obscene easter egg had gotten into that game. With a security system I planned to sell to the Justice Department, however, I'd felt it necessary to go over every line myself before running a trial.

I'd been prepared to install the system on my own server to see how it worked and to use as an example to the Justice Department. If a company wasn't willing to use its own products, something was wrong. It was a good thing I hadn't done that first.

I scowled at the code someone had put into my program. A backdoor. And I wasn't naïve enough to think this was some innocent little prank to allow someone to mess around with the sprinkler system or something silly like that. No, this was the kind of backdoor people wrote to allow unfettered access to a company's systems. It would've been bad enough to allow someone access to Archer Enterprises. I didn't even want to think what would've happened if I'd sold the program to the government without catching the problem. Records wiped or altered. Cases thrown out. Criminals going free.

Ned, I knew, was innocent, but I had a suspect now. I'd originally thought Truman had simply missed Ned's messed up log-ins, but now the picture was growing clear.

Ned had said he'd had trouble with his log-ins and that Truman had helped him with its recovery.

While Truman might've had access to certain information about the other employees, no one had access to all the log-in information except me. Truman could reset things, but he couldn't steal the encrypted information. If he'd done something to mess up Ned's log-in, then offered to 'help' reset things, he could've easily learned Ned's passwords and other security questions during that time period. That would explain why he hadn't said anything about the overtime put in on the program.

I was half-tempted to just call the cops and have Truman arrested, but while I was nearly certain he was responsible, I didn't have one hundred percent proof. There was also always the possibility of extenuating circumstances. Despite what had happened with Lara, I always wanted to give people the benefit of the doubt, see the best in them. Or, honestly, maybe it was because of what had happened. She hadn't, after all, intended to hurt me. There had just been extenuating circumstances. Lara hadn't made me cynical about women or people in general, just about love. In fact, the two of us were friends again.

I made my decision and picked up the phone. "I'm having a problem with the security software I just installed. I need you to come to my office."

Less than fifteen minutes later, Truman was standing on the other side of my desk, his fingers nervously twitching against his leg. His eyes shifted back and forth, never landing on one particular spot for long. If I hadn't already thought him guilty, his behavior definitely would've made me suspicious.

"Were you here late with Ned Baker last Tuesday night?" I didn't want to dance around the topic, but I also didn't want to come right out and accuse an employee of illegal activity. I figured if I kept it vague, he might think that his misdirect with Ned had worked.

Truman shrugged. "Maybe. I'd have to check my time card."

"What about Thursday?" I asked, leaning back in my chair and trying to appear casual.

"I wasn't here with him," he said slowly. "But I saw him here when I was leaving."

"And what time was that?"

"Seven or eight," he said. "I was going for a beer with my brother. I can give you the number if you want."

I stood. Truman wasn't a little guy, but I still had a couple inches on him, not to mention that a lot of his bulk was fat while I was muscle. I walked around the desk, unobtrusively pushing the intercom button. I'd made a call while I was waiting for Truman to come up.

"Did someone specific approach you, Truman, or did you come up with this idea all by yourself?" I stood a few inches away, looking down at him. "Because, you see, I don't think you're smart enough to have done this alone. You had to have had help. Tell me who it is and maybe things will go easier for you."

Truman stood up and moved closer to me. A

smile crossed his face. "You think you're so smart," Truman sneered, surprising me with his contempt. "Looking down at all of us. No one can get one over on you." His smile grew bigger as he continued. "Well, you're not as smart as you think. Installing the security software was your biggest mistake. Before coming up here, I called my contact who's paying me good to use the little backdoor I created. Every code you own, every game, app and software from Archer's Enterprise has now been compromised and is in the hands of one your competitors. You'll be ruined."

I shook my head. "But I didn't install it, Truman. I just told you that I did."

In an instant Truman's smile vanished. His face turned pink, then red and he clenched his hands into fists.

"You really don't want to do anything else stupid," I warned him.

He growled and swung. I side-stepped easily and cracked him right in the jaw just as the elevator opened and a pair of cops stepped into my office. Truman staggered back, right into their waiting arms.

"He's all yours. Get him out of my sight," I said.

"Yes, Sir." The youngest of the officers nodded at me and then read Truman his rights as he cuffed him.

Once my office was empty again, I sank down in my seat. I'd have to address the company at some point to stifle the rumors I knew would be flying with gossip as juicy as this. But first, I needed a couple minutes. Not only because my hand was starting to hurt and I was still pissed off, but because I needed to figure out how much to tell them and what I planned to do next.

I had two part-time security techs, but they mostly worked weekends to keep an eye on anyone working overtime. I needed to replace Truman and fast. The thing was, he hadn't been that easy to find in the first place. It would take time to advertise, accept applications, review resumés, conduct interviews, narrow down a pool of candidates, do background checks, hire someone and then see if they were as good in real life as they were on paper.

I picked up the phone. I hadn't needed to hire anyone new since Curt had left and he'd been the one to handle all those things before. Maybe he'd have a name for me. If he didn't, I supposed I'd just have to deal with it.

Chapter 7

Curt did indeed have a name. Jenna Lang. And she wasn't just a name, he informed me. Apparently, she had her own company and glowing recommendations from a professor Curt and I had taken classes from in college.

"Why would someone with their own company want to leave it to come work as a security tech here?" I asked.

"I'm thinking you might want her to be more than a security tech," Curt said. "You've been doing this by yourself for a year and a half. You need someone who can take on more of the responsibility. Someone you can trust and who'll do a good job."

"You want me to hire some stranger to be my partner instead of replacing Truman?"

I could almost hear him rolling his eyes at me. "No, dumbass. I want you to hire her for the security position, but give her some extra responsibilities until you can see that she's as good as I'm saying. See where things go from there."

"I can't afford to take the time to train someone," I said. "I'd be taking a serious risk hiring her without knowing what she can do."

"It doesn't matter who you hire," Curt said. "You're going to have to wait to see how they handle things either way. It's not like you can just bring someone in when something goes wrong and hope they know what they're doing."

An idea popped into my head. It was a little crazy and would mean lying to people, but it might actually work. I didn't tell Curt though. I wasn't sure he'd approve.

I chatted with Curt a few minutes more, then turned my attention to the job ahead. I figured I might as well start with Curt's recommendation, so I pulled up her site on my computer.

Well-designed. No frills. Also no picture of her, which I thought was interesting, if not a bit strange. When Archer Enterprises had gone public, Curt had insisted my picture be on the website. When I'd asked why, he'd bluntly stated that I was better looking. Did the lack of a picture mean that Jenna didn't have anyone working for her attractive enough to be featured on the site? Not that it was important, but it did say something about her personality if she worried about things like that.

I began to read through the site. There was practically nothing personal about Ms. Lang other than the fact that she was a CSU graduate like me. I didn't remember a Jenna Lang in any of my computer classes, but that didn't necessarily mean anything. I checked the company address first and that's when things started to fall into place. It was an apartment building known for housing non-traditional and recently graduated students. She worked out of her home, which meant she probably had only one or two people working with her, if any. And she was probably young, hence the lack of picture. I'd had to fight to prove myself and I knew it'd be even harder for a woman, as unfair as I thought it was.

Was that why Curt had mentioned her, I wondered. Since I'd technically started Archer Enterprises out of my dorm room freshman year, did he think I'd be more likely to hire someone who reminded me of myself?

While I doubted I'd be inclined to such a thing, I had to admit that I was intrigued. I'd do a background check a bit later, but at the moment, I wanted to put a face to the name.

I started to get up, then remembered that everyone on the floors below were probably trying to figure out what was going on with Truman. I had to admit that I was a bit surprised that no one had come up to ask. Relieved, but surprised.

I quickly typed out an email to the whole company. I kept it simple, saying that Truman had been arrested for work-related crimes and that he was no longer employed here. I assured them all that no one had been in danger and that things were to progress as normal. I supposed it sounded a bit terse, but I wasn't exactly in an eloquent mood at the moment.

I hit send, waited a couple minutes to make sure that everyone had time to get their email alerts and then headed straight down to the lobby. I waited until I was outside and heading for my car before I called Christophe to let him know I was out of the building for a while. I could hear people buzzing in the background and got the impression that my email was making the rounds. To his credit, Christophe didn't ask any questions, but rather acknowledged what I'd said and ended the conversation.

I pulled up in front of the building not too much later, but I didn't get out of the car. I wasn't sure if I wanted to go in and introduce myself, then ask her to come in to interview, or if I wanted to take my time. I needed someone soon, but I also needed to be thorough. I could do the background check this afternoon, then put into motion the plan I'd come up with while on the phone with Curt.

It was actually pretty simple, aside from the deception part. I'd contact a potential employee and hire them to fix a problem. I'd spruce up Truman's backdoor, make it harder to find, and then tell the person a half-truth about what had happened. I'd make it sound like the program was already installed in my system and I only had a couple hours to get it fixed before Truman's client knew my company was vulnerable. I'd have to say someone else had found it to make it seem like I couldn't fix it myself. I didn't like the idea of anyone thinking I couldn't spot something like that, but it would be the only way the lie would work.

With this plan, I'd be able to see how someone would react in a high pressure, time sensitive situation, how thorough and fast they were and how dedicated. If they were good enough, I'd tell them the truth, and their reaction would tell me a great deal about their personality.

I pulled out my phone and looked at the number for Lang Tech Consulting. If Curt thought she was good, I'd start with his recommendation. As I dialed, I looked out the window. A figure caught my eye, and it was no wonder.

She was about average height with an athletic build that was worth a second look, especially in her short skirt and fitted shirt. And her hair was blue. Like bright blue. I could see some piercings glinting in the sun as well as some impressive ink. Definitely the kind of woman people looked at.

The phone in my hand started ringing and I watched as the blue-haired girl pulled hers out of her bag.

"Lang Tech Consulting."

Of course that would be her, I thought to myself with a smile. "Hi, I'd like to make an appointment," I said. "It's a big system job, so it'll need to run late when everyone's out of the office."

I watched her bend over and dig through her bag, pull out a notebook and ink pen. The skirt rode up her thighs, exposing the sleek muscles there. "That's fine," she said as she stood back up.

Her voice was a bit huskier than I'd imagined and my stomach twisted. I wondered what she would sound like in bed. Moaning. Calling my name...

"Sorry, could you repeat that?" Heat rose to my cheeks as I realized I'd completely missed what she'd said.

"What's the company name?" she asked again.

"Archer Enterprises." I watched as she disappeared into the apartment building. "And the sooner, the better."

I was tempted to drag out the conversation, but I decided against it. I'd have plenty of time to talk to her when she came in for her 'interview.' I fully intended to stay and watch her through the whole thing. Aside from needing to see how she worked and processed difficult situations, I also wasn't about to let some stranger anywhere near my system without me hovering over them. If she was as good as Curt claimed, she could do serious damage if she wanted to.

I watched the building for a few more minutes, then headed back to the office. I couldn't quite get her out of my head though. I wasn't sure what it was, but something about her intrigued me. Maybe it was because I wanted to know the story behind her appearance. The hair. The tattoos and piercings. The clothes. Who was this girl? What was her story?

– The End –

Don't miss the captivating final installment, Pure Pleasures; release May 26th.

Other book series from M. S. Parker

Sinful Desires Complete Box Set

Twisted Affair Complete Box Set

Casual Encounter Box Set

Forbidden Pleasures

Dark Pleasures

Pure Pleasures – release May 26th

French Connection (Club Prive) Vol. 1 to 3

Chasing Perfection Vol. 1 to 4

Club Prive Vol. 1 to 5

Acknowledgement

First, I would like to thank all of my readers. Without you, my books would not exist. I truly appreciate each and every one of you.

A big "thanks" goes out to all my Facebook fans, street team, beta readers, and advanced reviewers. You are a HUGE part of the success of my series.

I have to thank my PA, Shannon Hunt. Without you my life would be a complete and utter mess. Also a big thank you goes out to my editor Lynette. You make my ideas and writing look so good.